WALKING WITH
WEREWOLVES

CHELSEA MCGINLEY

WALKING WITH WEREWOLVES

This is a work of fiction. All of the characters, names, incidents, organizations, and dialogue in this novel are either the products of the author's imagination or are used fictitiously.

iUniverse books may be ordered through booksellers or by contacting:

iUniverse
1663 Liberty Drive
Bloomington, IN 47403
www.iuniverse.com
844-349-9409

ISBN: 978-1-6632-4756-8 (sc)
ISBN: 978-1-6632-4757-5 (e)

Library of Congress Control Number: 2023900612

Print information available on the last page.

iUniverse rev. date: 01/20/2023

Dedicated to my mom, who taught me everything I know, and my sister, who has always been my biggest fan.

CHAPTER 1

"I love you." My stomach clenches into a tight knot. That just fell out of my mouth. I didn't even think about it! How could I let that slip out like that?

Elias Thorn, my best friend of seventeen years, looks up from his meal, still chewing his last bite. He swallows. "What?"

I blush fiercely and drop my head, hoping my hair hides my face. "Nothing, just... thinking out loud."

He smiles brightly, his blue eyes dancing. "Your mind's always so busy. He stands up and takes his empty tray. "I'm heading to class. I'll see you after school."

I plaster a smile across my face as I look up. "You bet." Internally, I'm calling myself all sorts of names. Reckless, stupid, idiot. If he'd heard that, it would've ruined everything. Seventeen years of being best friends would've suddenly become so awkward.

As children, our parents would always tease us. "We know who you're going to marry," they'd say. Elias would always respond with some claim about it being gross. Outwardly, I would agree with him, but on the inside, I always thought how fun it would be to marry your best friend. We could have sleepovers all the time and we'd play together whenever we wanted. It's been a few years since our parents have mentioned it. I bet he still thinks it's gross.

We meet at my car at the end of the day. There's a small group of three or four girls that follow Eli out, whispering and giggling to each other while clearly checking him out. To his credit, he ignores them entirely. Eli is a very attractive guy. You'd have to be blind or dead to not notice him.

Not like me. I'm that weird girl in the corner that no one notices until they're tripping over her, literally. More than once people have tripped over me only to look surprised that I was standing there at all. Straight, black hair, mud-colored eyes, skin that's just a little too pale, whip-thin and barely a curve in sight. But Eli has always made me feel seen and as long as he sees me, it doesn't matter if the rest of the world thinks I'm invisible.

"Ready, Minny?" He asks. My name is really Amane, but Eli has always called me Minny. I think it's because he had trouble pronouncing Amane when he was little, and it just stuck like that.

"Yeah, just waiting for you."

He's quiet on the drive back to my house, staring out the window at the trees flashing by. "How's it going over there, Atlas?" I call him Atlas sometimes because he seems as though he's carrying the world on his shoulders. He says my brain is always busy, but I think his takes the cake.

He fidgets a bit. "Something doesn't feel right today."

"Maybe lunch was bad." I offer.

"I'm serious, Amane. Don't you feel it?" Now he's looking at me.

He really is serious if he's using my actual name. He's right though, something feels off. Growing up, our parents would tell us we were special. That's what all parents tell their children, but for us, it wasn't to make us feel good about ourselves. It was a warning. We were different and we knew it. With that warning came a list of rules. The first rule was, always trust your instincts.

Right now, our instincts scream that something isn't normal. It's hard to follow those instincts when they're so utterly vague, however. It's never felt like this before. It's always had a direction, something to pin it to. Now it's just 'something' and that non-descriptiveness of it is more unsettling than my prickling instincts.

"What is it?" I ask Eli.

He sighs, his fists clenching shut. "I don't know, but I don't like it." That's even more unsettling. As strong as my instincts are, Eli's are better. He's like an animal that knows when a storm is coming. He can feel it from miles away.

I pull into the driveway, and we walk into the house. Mom's just as chipper as always. Maybe she doesn't feel it. Maybe it's nothing. That's wishful thinking though, it's never nothing.

"Hey kids, how was school?" She asks with a smile.

"It was school," I answer in the same instant that Eli says, "Great!"

"Where's Dad?" I ask, heading for the stairs.

"Out back, fixing the firepit. Winter was not kind to it," Mom answers. Eli and I exchange looks. What's going on? Why aren't they reacting to the wrongness in the air?

I pause at the top of the stairs to listen. Mom's on the phone now. "The kids are here and safe," she's saying. "No, I don't think so. Yes, hurry. Good luck, Dorris."

Dorris is Eli's mom. So, they do sense what's happening! Why won't they tell us what's going on?

Eli takes my arm and drags me into my room. "Look," he says, jabbing a finger at the window. Below us on the grass, Dad is setting up stakes around the firepit, sharpened ends pointing skyward. "Were we just not supposed to notice that?" He whispers. I don't know why he's whispering.

"What's going on?" I ask without expecting an answer.

Eli drops his school bag and heads for my closet, pulling out my shotgun and twin pistols. I am aware that normal seventeen-year-old girls are not packing heat in their closets, but, like I said, I'm not normal. Our parents made it a group effort to teach us everything they know about self-defense from the time we were old enough to walk. They have never given us a clear reason why we needed to learn this stuff or why we're different. When we would ask, they'd always just say, "We'll tell you when you're older." I think right about now would be a good time to know.

"Here, take these." Elias hands me my pistols in their shoulder holster. "You're better with them than I am."

"Do you really think we'll need these?" I ask, strapping it on without waiting for an answer.

"I don't know, but it's best to be prepared." He's right. Just like the Boy Scouts, our parents drilled that into our heads. 'Always be prepared.'

"I could do a better job of it if they'd tell us what we're supposed to be preparing for," I grumble.

Eli flashes me that fabulous smile of his. "Isn't this more exciting, though?"

"No," I answer, even as I feel the excitement flutter through my insides.

The front door opens downstairs, and I poke my head out of my room to listen. Mom answers, "Dorris, you made great time! Kai is preparing some defenses in the back." Defenses for what?

"Where are the kids?" Dorris asks.

"Upstairs doing homework, I think."

"Do they know?"

"I'm sure they know something's going on, but I haven't said anything to them."

Eli sidles past me and heads for the stairs, shotgun in hand. His face is set in determination. I follow close behind. Halfway down the stairs he stops to face the conversing women and I have to stand on my tiptoes to see around him.

"What is it we don't know?" He asks. I don't think I've ever heard him sound so serious.

Both women turn and plaster smiles on their faces. "Elias, how was school, Sweetie?" Dorris deflects.

A muscle twitches in Eli's jaw. "What don't we know, Mom?"

"Don't worry about it, it's nothing, Hon. Why don't you two get back to your homework?"

I'm sure I'm feeling the same frustration until he actually growls, real low in his throat like a dog's warning. I've heard it before when we would argue as children. It always makes me pause and pull back. I've never been willing to push him past this warning.

I place my hand on his shoulder to calm him down, but he wrenches away. "Don't," he tells me through clenched teeth. Then, to Dorris and my mother, "don't lie to us. I think it's time we learned what's going on. Everything, from the beginning."

Dorris's smile changes into a scowl. "Don't you growl at me, Elias Wolfric Thorn. I am your mother, and I decide when and what to tell you."

Eli immediately backs down. His mother has always had that effect on him. She's a fierce woman with a tendency to become quite scary. I do my best to stay on her good side.

He lowers his eyes, and his shoulders slump as though all the air has gone out of him. "Sorry, Mom," he mumbles.

She softens, flashing me a smile. "Amane, can I borrow my son for a moment?"

I flush at the request. "Yeah, of course." Eli completes his climb down the stairs without lifting his head to look at Dorris. This day just gets weirder and weirder.

Mom looks up at me with a gentle smile. "Everything is going to be alright, sweetheart. We're going to take care of it. Please, just focus on your studies so you can do well on your finals. That's all you need to worry about."

"Yes, Ma'am." I want to believe her, but there's a feeling of dread gnawing at my insides.

It's almost a full twenty minutes before Elias returns to my room. He flops onto my bed as though he hasn't slept in days and curls up on his side; the shotgun gripped in both hands. I don't know why, but sometimes the conversations with his mother seem to exhaust him beyond all reason.

"Did you learn anything?" I ask.

He shakes his head. "Sorry, Minny," he mumbles. I smile at his apology. I know he's already asleep, so I ask no more questions.

The hours pass in a haze of tension and nerves as I wait for that mysterious 'something' to begin. Even supper is put off in lieu of more pressing matters. I attempt to focus on studying and homework, but my mind continuously wanders and time and again, I find myself staring blankly out the window.

The sun has been down for some time and the moon has begun its steady climb into the sky when Eli sits up suddenly and stares out the window. Every fiber of his being is tensed as he listens. I strain my ears also, but hear nothing.

"It's starting," he says quietly. And then I hear it, still far off, a wolf howls. Is that what woke him? How could he have possibly heard something so quiet while sound asleep?

The howls close in rapidly, faster than seems possible. Outside the window, Dad has lit a fire. A huge, leaping bonfire. It sounds like we're surrounded by wolves now. Why would they come so close to where humans live?

I head for the window, but Eli beats me to it, closing it and drawing the blinds. "Stay back. Don't let them see you," he warns.

"They're just wolves."

"They aren't wolves," he says. Confusion and curiosity surface in my mind, fringed in a sort of quiet anger. We don't have any secrets between us. That's the point of being best friends. But here he is, suddenly withholding information from me. Keeping secrets I feel I ought to know right about now.

"What are they?" I ask.

"Just stay down." Is his answer.

"Eli, I..." My words are cut off by a scream outside. "Mom!" I jump to my feet and Eli immediately pulls me back to the ground.

"Stay down," he repeats.

"What's going on?"

I guess he sees the fear in my eyes because he finally says something useful. Or at least it would be if it didn't come out of some fairy tale. "Werewolves."

I wrinkle my nose at him, thinking he's joking to ease the tension. "Werewolves aren't real." He doesn't get the chance to argue because the night is suddenly full of the sounds of snarling and fighting.

Terror floods through me when I realize he's not joking at all, and I duck my head and put my arms over it. The sounds outside fall silent abruptly. I wait the span of a breath, and then another. Slowly, I raise my head and meet Eli's eyes. Outside my bedroom door, the sound of a snuffling dog creeps through.

Eli rises slowly into a crouch, readying the shotgun. I follow suit with my pistols. The snuffling stops and the door eases open, creaking on its old hinges. Elias takes aim. An enormous wolf, man, thing bursts into the room and is immediately blown away by the shotgun.

In the same instant, my window shatters, spraying us with bits of glass as a clawed hand closes around my ankle. I scream for Eli, and shoot at the beast, but nerves and the act of being dragged have my aim off, and I hit it in the shoulder. It flinches but doesn't release me. I'm pulled up and over the windowsill, my hands trying frantically to get a solid hold on anything I can reach.

"Elias!" I scream again.

Until now, he's been busy keeping the door clear. Now he spins around, sees me clinging to the window with bits of glass digging into my palms, and yells for me. He attempts to shoot the werewolf, but the gun is empty. He flings it aside and grabs my hands.

The wolf is stronger, and my hands are now slick with blood from the glass. Eli's grip slips and for a split second our eyes lock as we realize exactly how this is going to end. His are glowing yellow! Then I slip through his fingers and I'm falling. He actually leaps out after me, transforming before my eyes. Claws grow where once there were fingernails, his face and body shifting, growing, until what lands on the ground is no longer Elias, but a werewolf.

CHAPTER 2

Elias barrels full speed into the beast holding my ankle and they fall back. The other werewolf barely has a chance to register what's happening before Eli tears its throat out with his teeth. I shudder at the sight, scrambling to my feet and drawing my second gun. There are three more werewolves surrounding us.

Eli backs up, so we're back-to-back. I know a sane person would run from such contact, but this is my best friend in the world. Werewolf or not, there's no one I would trust more at my back.

The wolf in front of me lunges and I squeeze off a shot, missing a killing mark yet again. The bullet stuns it but is otherwise harmless. It shakes it off and continues its charge, swinging a massive paw and knocking my gun from my grasp. I duck and roll, coming to my feet near the bonfire. I grab a stick that's only half caught and swing it just as the werewolf comes in for another attack.

It yelps and backs up, and then Eli's tearing into it. Again, the night falls silent. I'm breathing hard and waiting for the next attack to come at any second. Gradually, the ground around me comes into focus. There are at least a dozen dead werewolves littering the yard.

Then my eyes settle on something that makes my heart stop. "Mom, Dad!" They're laying side by side on the ground. There's so much blood. I know they're gone, but I just can't accept it until my hands are on them. "No, no, no! Mom? Mom!"

I can feel myself becoming hysterical and I don't know how to stop it. I shake them and scream their names, anything to make them wake up.

Dorris is gone as well. Another piece of my heart shattered. This was my family. Our family. What are we supposed to do without them? Just seeing them lying here makes the world feel somehow empty. Like there is a gaping hole where they once stood and lived and breathed, and now don't. It's a suffocating feeling. How do I fill that void?

Eventually, Eli comes to sit beside me and pulls me against him. At some point he changed out of werewolf form. What's left of his pants are in tatters. If they had actually fit rather than been slightly baggy, I can't imagine they would have survived the shift.

He just rocks me while I sob into his shoulder. He's crying too. I can feel it when he breathes, his body shudders. I don't know how long we stay like that, rocking and crying, but finally, we pull ourselves together.

"We need to get out of here," Eli says, pulling away and standing as he wipes a sleeve across his face.

"What about them?" I ask, waving a hand to take in the scattered dead werewolves.

"We'll burn them," he says.

"And... our parents?"

"Help me get them inside, all of them," he answers, moving to lift Dorris under the arms and drag her into the house.

"What?"

"We'll put them all in the house, then burn it down. With any luck, it'll just look like they died in a house fire." It seems morbid, but he's right. We can't have people looking into the battle wounds that actually killed them. No one would believe werewolves were behind this.

We get them inside and then gather supplies for our escape. In my bag I include both of my parents' journals and any backup ammo they had. Then Eli pours a trail of gasoline from the fire to the house and over the bodies before kicking some flaming wood onto it. I watch wordlessly, tears streaming down my cheeks as my home goes up in flames.

My home, my family, Dorris, in the blink of an eye, they've been taken from me, and I'm left with a meager bag of possessions and Elias. I quietly thank my ancestors that I still have Elias with me. He's the only thing holding me somewhat together.

9

He has to take my hand to lead me away. I'm grateful for that. I don't have to think or function, just put one foot in front of the other. He shows me to the passenger side of the car and makes sure I remember to buckle. That doesn't require thought either.

I know I should be asking questions; Where are we going? How long has he known about werewolves? When did he become one? What are we supposed to do now? But my mind is in a fog, and I can't seem to grasp any of them tightly enough to force them through my lips.

I stare dumbly at my hands until the car comes to a rolling stop. When I look up, I see Eli's house. I can't make my brain understand why we are here, even though it's obvious. Where else would we go?

He unbuckles and climbs out. "Wait here, I'll be right back," he says.

Panic suddenly grips me at the thought of being alone. "Why? Why aren't we staying?"

"We can't stay. I just need to grab a couple of things."

"I'm coming with you." It's childish, but the thought of being alone right now is terrifying. I was useless against those beasts back there. If Eli hadn't been there, I'd be dead too.

He doesn't argue, so I trot after him into the house. I sit on his bed while he crams clothes and things into his bag. My mind is starting to clear, somewhat, as the initial shock wears off.

"You have blood on your face," I point out.

He looks at me as though I'm speaking another language, then understanding sets in and he blushes and looks away. "Sorry," he mutters, dropping his bag to wash up in the bathroom. Images of our short battle flash through my head. He actually used his *teeth* to rip their throats out. A shudder runs through me.

When he returns, he brings the first aid kit with him and sets it down on the bed beside me. Without meeting my eyes, he cleans my wounds from the glass and bandages them as best he can. "So… You're a werewolf?" I ask.

"Yup." He won't look at me.

"Since when?"

"Since birth."

"Oh."

He stops to look at me. There's concern in his eyes, and... fear? "Are you afraid of me now?"

I can see him actually harden himself before I answer. His muscles tense and his chest stops moving to take in air. I make sure to hold his gaze as I answer, willing him to believe me. "No, never."

His breath whooshes out in relief and the corner of his mouth quirks up in a half smile. "Thank you." He places the first aid kit into his bag and gives his room one last glance to see if he forgot anything. "Ok, let's go."

"Where are we going?" I ask as I follow him out of the house.

"To find my father."

"Your father?" All this time, I assumed Eli's father was dead. Now, I learn he's just a deadbeat. "Are you going to explain this to me, or do we have to play twenty questions all night?"

He actually chuckles at that. "No, I'll tell you what I know once we're on the road."

True to his word, as soon as we've merged onto the interstate, he explains. Sort of. "Do you know what today is, Minny?" He asks.

"Sure, April twenty-eighth. Why?"

"It's my birthday," he says with a smile.

I shake my head. "No, it's not. Your birthday is in July. July ninth." It's so close to mine that our parents usually rolled them into one day.

"Yeah, that's what my mother told everyone. Even my birth certificate says as much, but it's a lie. I was born on this day eighteen years ago."

"Care to elaborate?" I press.

"Somewhere around twenty years ago, my mom met a man in a steakhouse. She was a waitress, and he was a customer. He asked her out. They fell in love and then Mom became pregnant. That's when my father came clean about what he really was, a werewolf. He wanted Mom to abort, said this was no world for a half-breed. Mom refused. She told him she loved him anyway and loved the part of him growing inside of her.

11

"So, deciding I'd never be safe as long as he stuck around like a bright red beacon to other werewolves, Dad packed up and left. He cut all ties to the family he'd built. He didn't even tell Mom where he was going. For her part, Mom delivered me at home with only your mom there to help her. When she had my birth certificate made, she lied about the date of birth and gave me her last name.

"Mom told me all this because I needed to know what I was. Just before the full moon every month, I get an injection that suppresses my werewolf half. The side effect is, I'm knocked out for roughly twelve hours. Mom was late tonight, which is why I was getting so worked up on the stairs. It didn't matter, anyway. It didn't work this time.

"About a month ago, Mom received a letter from a mysterious source. It just said, 'He's of age. They will come.' Mom shut down after that and wouldn't tell me anything, but my guess is those werewolves were coming for me. They could smell me just as well as I could smell them."

He falls silent. I sift through this new information. That's a lot to take in. His parents must have loved him an incredible amount to give up everything, including each other, in order to keep him safe. "Why do you think the shot didn't work?"

He shrugs. "Beats me. Maybe at eighteen, the wolf blood gets too strong."

"Do you think the letter came from your father?"

"Without a doubt." He gives me a sideways glance, as though unsure about saying what he's about to. "When I was a baby, my mom used to wrap me in a shirt he had left behind. It still smelled like him, like sun-warmed earth and cloves. She said I always stopped crying when I was in that shirt. That's how the letter smelled, just like Dad."

I blink in astonishment. "You still remember the smell of an old shirt?"

He nods. "I still remember lots of smells from back then."

"Do you know how to find him now?"

There's a long pause and he won't meet my gaze. "Not exactly, no."

"Great! So, we're just speeding off to no man's land without any type of plan or destination?"

"No," he balks. "I have a destination in mind. I thought we'd start in the town we were born in, see if we can pick up a trail there."

We were born in a small town in the foothills of Mount Elbert in Colorado. About a year after our birth, we all moved to Montana and settled in the country at the base of the Rockies. I guess I never put much thought into it, but it is strange our parents seemed to make a group decision to all move to a new town. Most grown-ups don't move just because their friends are moving.

I mutter to myself, but a better plan doesn't come to mind. "Fine," I concede.

"You should get some sleep. Something tells me there's not going to be a lot of time for that soon," he advises. I oblige, realizing just how tired I am as soon as my eyes close.

When I wake, the sun is on its way up and we're pulling into a gas station. "Where are we?" I ask.

"Wyoming, about halfway to our destination, I believe."

"Do you want me to drive the next half? You must be exhausted."

He gives me a half smile. "That would be awesome, honestly. I've been head bobbing for the past hour."

I frown at him. "You should have woken me."

"You tend to punch me when I wake you."

I roll my eyes. "It's better than dying. Honestly, a big, tough werewolf afraid of being hit by a girl."

"You hit really hard," he protests, but he's smiling.

Eli's asleep before we've even returned to the interstate. It's a long, quiet drive and I feel almost guilty that I let him drive on his own for so long. The silence makes it difficult to keep the thoughts at bay and soon I'm fighting to hold back tears and see clearly. I never knew before that sadness could cause the heart to actually hurt.

I turn on the radio. It doesn't matter what's playing, anything to drown out my thoughts. Elias shifts in his sleep and I turn it down a bit and try to refocus my mind. One of my parents' rules in training was to focus on what was right when everything seems so wrong, so

I breathe and count my blessings. I'm alive, I still have Elias, the day is going to be sunny, my car is running, and we are fed and warm. I hit a mind block and start over, again and again, in an endless loop.

Eli wakes with a start three hours later and peers blearily around, like he doesn't recognize his surroundings, which, of course, he doesn't. "Bad dream?" I ask.

He yawns and stretches as much as the car will allow. "Yeah." He's looking at me intensely, as though he can see right into my brain. "Are you ok?"

That simple question breaks down my walls, and the tears burn behind my eyes again. "Yeah," I lie, before bursting into tears.

He's startled by such an extreme reaction. "Amane, pull over," he orders. I do as he says. I can tell he's struggling to find a way to comfort me. Honestly, I don't expect him to. He's never been good at handling my breakdowns.

He sits quietly until my sobs start to slow. Hesitantly, he reaches out to rub my back. "It's going to be ok," he says and immediately cringes at the words. How is any of this going to be ok? I have no home, no family to return to, and we're being hunted by werewolves, or at least he is. I've been sucked in by association. Not to mention we're on a wild goose chase to find a man that no one's heard from in almost nineteen years.

Despite the bleak outlook, I smile at his poor attempts at comfort. "You suck at this."

"Yeah, I think we've established that in the past." He drops his hand into his lap and looks out his window before turning back to me. "Maybe it's lame to say, but Mom used to tell me that as long as you and I have each other, we have a home and a family."

"What about her?"

He shrugs. "I think she always expected to… die young. Maybe she knew the werewolves would get her one day. She was always saying stuff like that. Like, 'Be nice to Minny, you never know when she'll be all you have', or, 'Remember to watch Minny's back, someday you might be the only one who can.'"

I stare out the windshield. "My parents say... said the same thing, 'Elias may be all you have one day.' Do you think they knew this would happen?"

"Maybe. Maybe they were just preparing us for the worst."

"Oh, so now I'm the worst?"

His mouth drops open to protest, but stops when he realizes I'm teasing him. He props his chin in his hand, elbow resting on the door handle, and looks out his window. "Well, you're not the best," he mocks.

I fake gasp and punch his arm. "Like you're a treat to be stuck with."

"Ow! See, beating on me already," he says, rubbing his arm and grinning. "Seriously though, I can't think of anyone I'd rather be left with."

I wipe my face again and sniffle. "Same here," I answer. Feeling somewhat better, I maneuver back into the lane.

Eli reaches back over the seat and pulls my bag out, opening it to rummage around. "What are you looking for?" I ask.

"The ammo you packed. I just want to see what our stash looks like. I'm hoping what you grabbed will keep us going for a while."

"There are other options, I suppose. Crossbow, sword, lance..." I have no experience with a lance. I'm not even sure they're made anymore, but the idea is driving a wooden stake through the werewolf, so any long piece of sharpened wood would do.

"That's true," Eli agrees. "How much money do you have?" He's pulling out the boxes of ammo now.

"Five or six hundred, I think."

He gives me a sharp look. "You *think*? You don't know what you have in your bank account?"

I shrug. "I know estimates. I had roughly twenty-five hundred before I bought the car. It cost fifteen hundred, plus insurance and registration, then the snow tires." That was maybe two thousand one hundred in the end. There's been a few paychecks since then, among other expenses.

"Minny, that was almost five months ago. Have you looked at your account since then? You've been paid at least nine times."

I blush at my foolishness. "No, I guess I haven't. How much do you have?"

It's his turn to blush. "Three hundred and change."

"Seriously? What happened to your savings?"

"Nothing," he mutters, separating the boxes of bullets into two groups.

I give him a hard look. "You bought another gun, didn't you?" Ordinarily, it wouldn't matter. What he does with his money is his business, but right now we really could have used some shared savings.

"So? Clearly, we needed it," he answers defensively.

"And where is it now, Eli?"

"At home," he mumbles, looking at his lap. The situation is just too ridiculous for me to even be upset. I start laughing. A fine pair we are, all that training and we skipped the second most important rule; *Always be prepared.*

Eli smiles, setting three boxes of bullets onto the back floorboards. "Ok, so neither of us is great with money management. I'll monitor the accounts and you make sure I don't buy something stupid. Deal?"

"Deal." That's easier said than done. He'll make all sorts of excuses if he sees something he really wants, regardless of its level of usefulness.

"These two are the rounds for the shotgun." He's repacking the remaining two boxes. "The three in the back are for the pistols. Try to aim better in the future. We need to make these last."

I roll my eyes at him, but my heart drops a bit at his words. I failed hard back there. That can't happen again. I need to keep my wits about me.

His decision that we need all those bullets prompts a question, however. "How many enemies do you expect to see where we are going?"

He shrugs. "No clue, but better safe than sorry."

CHAPTER 3

Three and a half hours later, we pull into the town of our birth. It's only a little bigger than the town we grew up in. Eli has his head out his window like a dog, tracking down a scent I can't even remember.

He sits back after a few minutes, his hair hilariously disheveled. "Turn left ahead."

"Where are we headed?" I ask, maneuvering through the first left I come to."

He grins at me. "Home!" He guides me back out of town and down a winding back road until we come to an old farmhouse.

I pull into the driveway and shut off the engine. "This is your old house?" It comprises three sections, each one clearly added at a later date than the last as an extension. The roof is covered in tin, red with rust and age. The walls are a faded gray, which suggests it was once white.

"This is *our* old house," he answers, opening his door. "Shall we?"

I scurry out after him. "We're going in?"

"Of course. Where better to begin our search than the beginning?" I guess that's a good point. I'm still not comfortable just marching into some stranger's house, though.

"I had no idea we all lived together back then," I think out loud.

Eli marches right up to the door and knocks as though this is all perfectly normal. A solid-looking woman answers with a scowl. Her broad build and wide stance make it clear no one is getting past her. I shift slightly, so Eli's between us. She looks more than capable of throwing us off her steps if she chooses. "I'm not interested," she says immediately.

"Sorry, what?" Eli asks politely.

"Whatever you're selling, I'm not interested."

"We're not selling anything," he tells her. "We were actually born here and were hoping to see it. Take a walk down memory lane, so to speak."

"And I'm just supposed to buy that pile of horseshit? For all I know, you kids are planning to rob me blind." She crosses her arms and juts one leg off to the side. A stance Dorris took often when she was in no mood to be messed with.

Elias throws a 'help me' look over his shoulder at me. I sigh inwardly and step forward. "Please, ma'am, we lost our home and our parents in a terrible fire, and this is our last connection to them. We won't touch anything, honest." It helps that a few very real tears well up in my eyes.

The woman softens a fraction but doesn't move. "I've been here a long time now. Who exactly were your parents?"

"Dorris Thorn and Kai and Melinda Ichinose," I answer.

She eyes us another moment and then breathes out a sigh and shifts aside. "Alright, you have five minutes. Make it quick." She steps aside to let us in.

Eli smiles broadly. "Thanks. We won't forget your kindness."

I don't have any memories of this place, seeing as I was barely a year old when we moved, but Eli seems to have very distinct memories of certain scents. I watch as he wanders through the rooms, trying not to look like he's sniffing everything. I can't shake the image my head has formed of him shuffling around on all fours like a hound tracking a fox.

His nose leads us to the back door. "Do you mind if we go out back? We spent a lot of time out there when we lived here," he says to the woman.

"Yeah, fine, but you've got ninety seconds left," she answers. A minute and a half to find a trail that's eighteen years old. Elias better have one hell of a sniffer.

We make it to the edge of the woods before the woman tells us our time is up. "Bit of a stickler, isn't she?" I comment.

Eli shrugs. "This is her home. She just wants to be safe, I'm sure."

We thank her profusely as we are leaving. She actually wishes us luck and smiles as we leave. An expression that brightens her entire demeanor.

Once we're down the road, I ask Eli if he found anything. He shakes his head. "Nothing fresh. My gut says we're going to have to head into the mountains, but we're going to go on foot, and I want to make sure we're properly prepared. We should get some food and other supplies today, find a hotel to stay in tonight, and start out early tomorrow morning."

It sounds like a good plan to me. It takes the rest of the day to find and pack everything we need for climbing a mountain. We won't be taking any of the usual trails, so safety gear was on the top of the list, closely followed by food. Everything we brought from home is re-evaluated for usefulness for the trek ahead. Anything that doesn't make the cut, we leave in my car for safekeeping.

The hotel room is cheap and dingy, but clean. We take turns showering, since we don't know when our next chance to take one might be. Elias goes first and by the time I'm done with mine, he's fast asleep on his bed. Not quite ready for sleep yet, I open my mom's journal.

There were a couple of reasons behind grabbing my parents' journals before burning the house down. One was for sentimental reasons. I wanted to have some connection to my parents still and what better way than knowing and understanding their deepest emotions? The second reason was in hopes of finding some answers to all of the questions I had that night and, the ones I've developed since.

Mom's journal doesn't provide too many answers. It tells of her friendship with Dorris, which spans into her youth, and of her meeting Dad. I skip the weird, mushy stuff, but read the part of their actual meeting. She mentions being on a hunt. What type of hunt is not stated. After that it's just normal, Mom stuff, all her fears and worries for my future and Eli's.

Dad's journal is far more informative. His very first entry tells what he was and about his life leading up to that point, as though he was writing it for someone else to read. He was a werewolf hunter, born to werewolf hunters. He'd spent his childhood being trained by his parents to eventually follow in the family business. He met Mom on a werewolf hunt when he was twenty-two and five years later, I was born.

From their first meeting, Mom, Dad, and Dorris agreed to stick together. They were stronger as a unit then and when Eli and I came into the picture it was clear that our futures would require them to be at their strongest. He hints at a fourth team member, but no name is mentioned anywhere in the journal.

At first, Dad's mind was only on the protection of the newborn half-breed, but then I was born, and his focus shifted entirely. When I was born, he realized he would do anything and everything to ensure my safety. He still cared for Elias, but if throwing him to the wolves, literally, meant I would survive then he believed he would do it.

Then I find an entry addressed specifically to me. Why he never gave it to me is a question I will probably never learn the answer to. The date at the top tells me it was written nearly ten years ago. I take a deep breath to steady my nerves and gather my courage before pressing on.

To my dearest little girl,

I am writing this letter in hopes that you will better understand all that you are meant to be. You are a very gifted child with abilities and talents that have not been seen among our people for many years. Someday you will surpass us all. I can feel it in my bones.

I know your mother and I push you hard in your training and you wish we would play normal games more often. I know this makes it difficult for you to make friends at school, not knowing the games they play, but you were born into a dangerous life. Everything we do, we do to keep you safe. One day, we may not be here to protect you anymore, and then it will be up to you.

I write this letter as a warning. Your mother insists I'm wrong, that this boy is different. I know he is your best friend, and perhaps part of that is our fault. Had you lived a more normal childhood, maybe you would have had more friends to cling to. I know you would go to the ends of the Earth for him, but sometimes our greatest allies become our greatest enemies.

Sweetheart, there may come a day when Elias becomes a threat to you. I need you to be strong and to keep an eye on him. He is not like you. He is a cross between our closest ally and our worst enemy and I don't know yet which path he will choose. I have seen how he loses his temper at times, and I just want you to be careful.

You, my child, are destined to be a great werewolf hunter, yet the fates have found it amusing to place the son of one of the strongest werewolves of our world, center stage in your life. Tread with caution and remember to always trust your instincts. Your heart may lie, but your gut never will.

Love, your superhero

When I was little, my dad used to read me superhero stories at bedtime, when I wasn't being told werewolf stories. I always said he was my superhero. I knew even then that Dad would move mountains if it meant it would keep me safe.

I also trusted my father more than anyone else in the world. The fact that he was so uncertain about Elias makes me wonder if I really should keep an eye on him. Guard my back against the one person who has always watched it for me. It's too much for my tired mind to want to consider currently.

I tear the letter out, fold it and stash it in my backpack. Then I shake Eli awake to show him my other findings. He's just as surprised as I was to learn that our parents were werewolf hunters. What's more interesting is that werewolf hunters don't seem to be entirely human. Or maybe, they are more evolved humans.

The journals tell of our heightened senses and our faster reflexes compared to a typical human.

The last thing we manage to glean from the journals, is our parent's desire for us to graduate high school before being thrown into the life of hunters. "I guess that didn't work out as planned," Eli remarks.

"We're not hunters yet," I argue.

"That's true. They make it sound like we won't have a choice, though. Like, once we're old enough, that's it. No more free will in our career paths." I'm quiet for a long time until Eli asks if I'm ok.

"It's just… well… you're half werewolf. Do you think I would have the choice to not hunt you if it came to that?"

"Let's hope so," he answers with a teasing smile. "I certainly don't want to die at your hands unexpectedly."

"Who says I'll win?"

He lays back against his pillows and closes his eyes. "You're being modest, Minny. We both know you're a more agile fighter than I am. Besides, I'd do my best to incapacitate you if we were in a fight. I'd never forgive myself if I actually hurt you."

I lay down in my bed. "Maybe." He's always been stronger than me, but I'm faster. It's the only reason I usually win in practice fights. I've never fought him in his werewolf form, though. I'm almost positive he would win, hands down, and I'm not so certain he would hold back in that form.

CHAPTER 4

We're woken by a knock on the door the next morning. Eli yawns and stretches before standing to answer it. "Probably housekeeping," he mumbles.

He opens the door and immediately steps back with his hands in the air. "Woah there fellas, it's a little early for guns, don't you think?"

Three men file in after him, two with guns aimed straight at his chest. Two of the men are in their forties, at least. The third doesn't look much older than us.

I freeze halfway out of bed, unsure if I should keep moving or not. The man in front nods toward me. "Both of you take a seat, hands where I can see them."

Eli backs up next to me and scoots onto the bed, slowly lowering his hands until they're resting on his legs. "I'm very sorry officers, but I think you have the wrong people." There's a hint of sass in his tone, but they don't seem to notice. I don't believe they're cops. None of them are wearing badges or uniforms.

"Shut up," orders the man who told us to sit as he moves towards our bags. I can see Eli struggling to hold his tongue. He's never been one to know when to shut up and it's gotten him into more than one fight at school.

The man pokes through our things while the other two keep their guns on us. Eli's leg starts jiggling and I know it's taking all of his self-restraint to not make a sarcastic remark. And then he caves, despite the warning look I'm giving him.

"Check the front pocket. That's where she usually keeps her menstrual supplies."

I don't think I've ever blushed faster or darker. I'd kick him if I didn't think it would get me shot. The man looks up in confusion. "Pardon?"

Eli shrugs nonchalantly. "I just assumed you might need some. Can't think of another reason you'd be so pissy this early in the morning." He looks at me then. "You've got some Midol in there, right?"

I look at my lap, clenching my hands together in an attempt to not lash out. Does he have a death wish or something?

The man's jaw visibly tightens, but there's a glimmer in his eyes that suggests he's holding back a smile. He rises to his feet and meets Eli's gaze squarely. "We have some questions for you two. I advise you to answer honestly."

There's a long pause before Eli nods. "Shoot. We have nothing to hide." I cringe at his choice of words.

"Yesterday, we tracked you to an old farmhouse. The woman there told us she was visited by an Elias Thorn, and Amane Ichinose. That would be you two, correct?"

"What of it?" Eli asks. I'd like to know why they were tracking us, or how they even knew we were in town.

The man ignores Eli's bratty reply and presses on. "Would you be the son of Dorris Thorn, and daughter of Kai and Melinda Ichinose?" Elias and I exchange looks. How do these people know our parents?

Eli crosses his arms over his chest and looks back at the man. "Who's asking?"

Now the three men exchange looks. "Just some old colleagues of theirs'."

"Colleagues with names? Or do you just go by Things One, Two and Three?" Eli presses.

There's that glimmer again. The man points at the first man who had entered our room. "John, Tony, and Langley." He indicates himself last. "Can we have an answer now?"

Eli glances at me again. I nod, hoping they know something more about our parents, or possibly something about Eli's father. "Yeah, they're our parents."

John releases a long, hissing breath. "I didn't know Dorris had any children."

Tony's eyes narrow at us with suspicion. "No one did."

"Except, apparently, Kai and Melinda," Langley adds.

"Surprise!" Eli says, wiggling his fingers in a wave.

"I'm sorry, who are you guys, exactly? Our parents never mentioned any colleagues." *Unless you count the three of them and their mysterious fourth team member.*

They lower their weapons at Langley's hand gesture, and he answers. "Werewolf hunters. And you two are coming with us."

Eli laughs. "Yeah, ok. Come on, Minny, let's hop into a car with a bunch of strangers brandishing guns."

The men frown at each other. "What my friend here is trying to say is no," I tell them.

"Yeah, we got that," Tony snaps.

"It wasn't a request, however," Langley continues. "Whatever you two are up to, I can guarantee you are underprepared. Your parents would never forgive us if we just let you run off willy-nilly."

"And I'd rather not be on the receiving end of Kai's or Dorris's tempers," John adds.

Eli shoves off the bed and walks over to Langley to retrieve our bags. "You're in luck then. They're dead," he says it so coldly and bluntly, I actually flinch. He hands me my pack. "Come on, we should get going."

"What do you mean, dead?" Langley asks.

"Did I stutter?" Eli growls, all signs of his previous sarcasm gone. They've pushed his buttons too far.

Langley looks at the ceiling and clenches his eyes shut like he's fighting back physical pain. And it is a kind of physical pain, this ache in my chest where Dorris and my parents once were. When he looks back at us, his eyes are glassy with unshed tears. "How?" His voice catches slightly in his throat.

"How do you think?" Eli demands, the other man's pain lost on him.

I place a hand on his arm to settle him. This isn't the time to be rude. Clearly, Langley is deeply upset by the loss. "It was werewolves. They attacked my home the night before last. Eli and I barely made it out alive," I explain gently.

"And now you're after revenge?" John asks.

"Do we look stupid?" Eli snaps back. "We're well aware we can't take on an entire pack of werewolves ourselves. We're looking for my father."

Langley looks at him sharply. "Who is your father?"

"That'd be nice to know, wouldn't it? If you'll excuse us." Eli shoulders past him and I follow behind. Tony grabs his arm on the way by and Eli immediately drops into self-defense mode, twisting around so the man is forced to let go. The twist is closely followed by a fist to Tony's gut, causing him to double over.

John grabs me from behind and fire crackles in Eli's eyes. He draws a gun from the back of his pants and shoves it at Tony's face. "Drop her or Tony dies." It's the last thought I should expect to have under the circumstances, but I can't help thinking about the fact that he must have slept with that pressed against his back. How was that possibly comfortable?

John responds in kind, pressing his own gun to my temple. "Is that a game you really want to play, boy?"

Eli's eyes harden as pulls the hammer back. "I'm fairly certain you're more attached to Amane than I am to Tony," he answers.

No one moves for what feels like an eternity. Then, I feel John sigh, his breath fluttering my hair. He releases me. "Fine, you win."

Eli lowers his weapon, disengaging the hammer. I shove him hard. "What the Hell, Elias? Don't you ever gamble with my life again!"

His answer is to pull me against his chest and hug me hard. I realize he's trembling. He was actually scared. Elias, who doesn't scare. "I'm sorry," he whispers, pressing his face into my neck.

I give him an answering squeeze before he lets me go and leads me out the door. Halfway to the car he stops, heaves a sigh, and turns back. "Fine, we'll go with you. Only because we're bound to run across werewolves and you're right when you say we're underprepared, but if any of you so much as throw Amane a dirty look, you *will* regret it."

The three men nod. "Fair enough. We'll take my car," John replies. After verifying there's nothing we need in my car, we pile into John's. The hotel is regularly used by hikers and campers, so my car should be fine here for however long we're in the mountains.

Elias holds his hand out to shake Tony's. "Sorry about that, man. No hard feelings, I hope."

Tony accepts the hand. "A man's gotta do what he's gotta do to protect his girl."

"She's not my girl," Eli answers automatically. I know I'm not, but it still hurts that he's so quick about shutting the notion down. "But she is all I have left in this world." Admittedly, that softens the hurt feelings some.

CHAPTER 5

I thought we were already in the middle of nowhere, but the longer we're in the car, the farther from civilization we seem to get. My mind starts to whir into second-guessing our decision until I'm on the verge of panic. What were we thinking, climbing into a car with three strange men? They could be taking us anywhere. They could be planning to kill us and drop our bodies in the woods, never to be seen again. And who would miss us? No one, that's who.

I close my eyes and take a few steadying breaths before I free fall into panic mode and throw myself out of a moving vehicle. *Always trust your gut.* Right now, contradictory to my spinning thoughts, my gut says to trust these men. And it's also reminding me I skipped breakfast.

"Where exactly are you taking us?" I ask.

"Hunter's Headquarters," Tony answers.

"Is it far?"

"Another half hour or so. Why?"

Before I can answer, my stomach lets out a rather loud rumble. Elias and Tony both turn to stare at me. I blush and look at my hands, clearing my throat. "No reason."

In the front passenger seat, Langley chuckles as he opens the glove compartment. He passes back a bag of trail mix. "We'll get you something more substantial once we get there."

"Just what is it that hunters do, exactly?" I ask, thinking this time in the car is as good as any to find out more about who I am.

Langley turns and pins me with a disbelieving stare. "Didn't your parents tell you?"

I shake my head, feeling defensive that he may think less of my parents. He rubs a hand over his face with a heavy sigh. "The easy answer is that we hunt werewolves," he says. "We have a set of rules, or a code that we try to live by, but there are those of us who may ignore the code and simply kill whatever werewolf they run across."

"And what is this code?" I ask.

"Essentially, we protect those who can't protect themselves. We are the ones who stand between killer werewolves and the rest of the world," Langley answers. That's a relief. No one is going to expect me to kill Elias simply because he is a werewolf.

Just as Tony predicted, we pull off the road roughly thirty minutes later. There're maybe five other cars parked nearby, but there's nothing else here. No buildings, trails, or even a sign to tell you where you might find something.

"Cool office," Eli comments. "Are we early, or is this the whole party?"

Langley no longer tries to conceal his humor at Eli's sarcastic remarks. "Most of us use the parking garage," he answers with a smile. "We're going to use the main entrance, however." I refrain from stating the obvious; there's *nothing* here.

He leads the way into the trees, with each of us trailing behind him. We come to a halt in front of a tree that doesn't stand out at all. Especially compared to the others surrounding it, in my opinion. John reaches out to touch a piece of bark and then we just stand there. I almost bail when a grinding noise stops me. It sounds like gears working.

The front of the tree slides open, revealing a completely hollow center. I know my jaw has hit the ground, but I can't seem to pick it up. Eli and I both stand there gaping at it until Langley ushers us forward. "Load up, kids."

Cautiously, I test the platform inside the tree, positive it's going to fall away under the barest of touches. It's solid. Eli, trusting my judgment and the fact that I haven't already plummeted to my death, steps in beside me. The other three men join us, and the tree slides closed again, shutting us into complete darkness. My hand automatically goes to my belt knife.

And then we're plummeting down through the dark. My breath catches as my free hand flies out, looking for some source of stability. It finds someone's back. "Steady," Langley's voice tells me.

Before crashing into the ground, the platform slows down and eases to a halt. "I'm not sure I care for the front entrance," Eli says as another door opens. He looks a little green from the experience.

John chuckles as he leads the way off the platform. "You get used to it." What lies before us looks like something straight out of a spy movie. There are people all over the place, bustling about like their lives depend on it. There are people at desks and people with gadgets and people around a water cooler. The sounds of wooden practice weapons colliding and shouts drifts in through a side door. It's a bit overwhelming. I'm certain my eyes are bugging out of my head.

A pretty blond somewhere in her mid-thirties stops in front of us with a smile. "Good morning John, Langley. Got some recruits there?"

"Something like that," John replies. "Would you excuse us, Tanya? We have a meeting with Benjamin."

"Yes, of course. Will I see you at lunch?" She asks.

"Perhaps," he answers. She flashes another smile at John and hurries about her business. Langley makes a sound in his throat as John leads us toward another door. "Shut up, Langley," he grumbles. Langley smiles mischievously.

"Did anyone else notice Tanya blatantly ignoring Tony?" Eli asks.

Tony shrugs with a grin. "We're lucky she noticed anyone other than John."

I'm completely enthralled by our surroundings as we're led down a corridor with several smaller offices, what appears to be a break room, and a handful of doors shut against prying eyes. All of this carefully chiseled out of the rocks that form the mountain.

We come to halt at the end of a long corridor and John knocks on this final door. "Enter," a voice answers. We step into an office to see a bald man sitting in a wheelchair behind his desk. My first impression of him is of Professor Xavier from the X-Men. The name plaque on the desk reads, *Benjamin W. Ludwig.*

Benjamin smiles brightly at us. "Gentlemen, welcome. What news do you bring?"

Langley takes the lead again. "Well, sir, do you want the good news first or the bad news?"

Benjamin considers for a moment. "Always best to end on a pleasant note. What is bad in our world today, young man?" Langley's easily in his forties, so it's funny to hear him addressed as a young man, even if Benjamin does look like he's mid-sixties.

"Dorris Thorn and her partners, the Ichinoses, are dead," Langley reports bluntly. I shift behind him, wondering when I'll get used to hearing those words.

Benjamin frowns. "That is most unfortunate."

"However," Langley plows ahead, clearly not willing to dwell. "We have located their children."

Benjamin's eyebrows shoot up. "No kidding! Where? I should like to meet them immediately."

Langley and John exchange looks. Apparently, Benjamin is not the brightest bulb in the box. "Right here, sir." Langley gestures at Eli and me.

"Oh, of course! Forgive me, I lose track of the faces that come and go after a while," Benjamin says. "Welcome to our little hideout." He smiles gently at us. "I'm sorry to hear about your mother and father."

Langley clears his throat. "The boy is Dorris's."

Benjamin's jaw drops. "No kidding? I never knew she married." I refrain from rolling my eyes. How many times are we going to go over this?

After a few more minutes of speculation and discussion over the men's travels, we're dismissed. John and Langley slip away on other business and Tony is advised to take us to the training room.

The training room is even bigger than the main office and there are people filling this room also, although I imagine it seems like there's more since they're dueling each other, working out, or generally being active. There are even children about, getting similar training to what Eli and I grew up with. Tony gives us a full tour of the equipment, including a shooting range and weapons room. I just can't seem to wrap my head around the fact that this is all underground.

"This is amazing," I breathe.

Tony smiles proudly, as though he dug the entire thing out himself. "And now you have open access to it all." My stomach growls again then, reminding us all that we still haven't had a decent breakfast. Tony looks sheepish. "Sorry, I forgot. Follow me."

The room attached on the other side of the training room is a large cafeteria. There's just a small trickle of people here, lingering over their breakfasts. Tony leads us to a small buffet. Based on the number of people here I had anticipated a larger spread, but I'm too hungry to be disappointed by the limited selection. There are bowls cooked oatmeal with honey, maple syrup, or brown sugar for sweetening. Along with a fruit bar and scrambled eggs.

I eagerly help myself to a bowl of oatmeal drizzled with honey and sprinkled with raisins. On a small plate I place a small serving of scrambled eggs. I get foggy halfway through the morning if I don't include some protein with my breakfast. Elias foregoes the oatmeal and fills his bowl with eggs, grabbing an apple before following Tony and me to a table. I may get foggy, but Eli gets downright mean without protein.

"No eggs for you?" Eli asks, glancing at Tony's meager helping of oatmeal.

Tony shakes his head. "I'm a vegan."

Eli starts to snicker and abruptly tries to cover it with a cough. "That's cool," he gasps out as I pat his back. I'm a little more aggressive than necessary, but he can be such an ass sometimes.

We're joined by a curly-haired brunette with honey-colored eyes. If I had to guess, I'd say she's no older than eighteen. She slides in next to Tony with a bright smile. "Who are your new friends, Antonio?"

Tony introduces us, and she shakes our hands. She leans one arm on the table and twirls her hair with her finger as her eyes single out Eli. "It'll be so good to have more fighters on our side."

I roll my eyes and focus on my oatmeal. Even hidden deep underground, he gets hit on by random girls. Tony catches my eye and gives me a sympathetic smile. I guess I'm not the only one completely ignored because of the company I keep.

Eli and our new companion, Sierra, keep up an animated conversation throughout the meal. Tony excuses himself first to take care of other things, leaving Sierra to finish our tour. I follow behind, trying not to notice the way she's looped her arm through Eli's. This isn't my first time as the third wheel when other girls set their sights on my friend. I do my best to shove my jealousy into the deep, dark corners of my heart, knowing he'll never see me as more than a friend.

We're introduced to a whirlwind of people. I'll never keep them all straight. That is, if I remember them at all. The day flies by as we're given the lowdown on the hunter's operations. Office workers who follow news reels and any other recordings available to the public that may lead to werewolves, hunters trained for field work, and students training for one position or another.

We are introduced to so many new people as well. After our third round of introductions, Elias takes to introducing himself as, "Elias Thorn, Dorris's son" and adding, "Yes, she had a child."

It seems our parents were well known here. Regarded as some of the most skilled hunters of their generation. A lot of people wondered where they had gone all those years ago. Some thought perhaps they had finally met their match among the werewolves. Eli and I greet this theory with half-hearted smiles and a distracted, "oh yeah?" I'm thankful for the speed in which these conversations move along, so we are not left dwelling on the accuracy of such statements for too long.

I glimpse John at lunch with Tanya, but other than that, I don't see our three original escorts at all. I'm a little peeved at being hauled here and dumped. Maybe I was mistaken when I assumed they were going to help us prepare for finding Eli's father.

There's a small section of the base carved out for bunk beds. Most of the hunters have their own homes, so the bunks are mostly used for those who need to remain hidden, or those like Eli and me who have nowhere else to go. Because of this, even though each room is equipped to house four occupants, Eli and I each get our own room.

Alone in my room that night, I'm assailed by images of my parents and Dorris lying dead on the ground, my house going up in flames, and the terrifying sight of werewolf claws closing around my leg. With the memories comes a daunting realization. All those werewolves had human forms and families somewhere, and we killed them.

The thought floods me with horror. They weren't just bloodthirsty beasts. They were intelligent beings and at least some of them had left behind families that are now mourning them.

My heartache shifts to anger. Unable to lie still, I push myself off the bed and begin to pace. It doesn't help to calm me at all.

Finally, I wrench my door open to storm across the hall and pound on Eli's. He opens his door a crack to peek out at me. "What's up?" He asks.

"I need to talk to you," I tell him, shoving past him and ignoring the fact that he's shirtless, until I see Sierra perched on the bed with only her bra covering her upper half.

Ordinarily, I might feel jealous or hurt and more than a little embarrassed. Right now, I'm a little too worked up to feel anything other than annoyed. I scowl at her. "I need to talk to Elias."

She smiles sweetly, making me want to smack her. "Ok." She makes no effort to leave.

"Amane, you can't just..." Eli begins to protest.

"Alone," I tell Sierra, cutting him off.

"As you can see, we're kind of in the middle of something, sweetie," she says in a condescending tone.

The last of my patience slips. I snatch her shirt off the floor and shove it into her arms before grabbing her arm to haul her out. "I don't give a shit! Get. Out."

She stumbles into the hall and turns a shocked expression on me as I slam the door in her face. "What the Hell, Amane!" Eli exclaims. "What the hell is your problem?"

"Elias, we're murderers!" Saying the words out loud breaks through my growing frustration, and a flood of tears presses against my eyes.

My outburst stops him cold. "What?"

"All those werewolves, dead at my house. They were people too, and we killed them all." Tears stream down my cheeks.

"Oh, Minny," Elias breathes, his own anger melting away as he pulls me into him. "They were going to kill us. We did what we had to in order to survive."

"I know," I sob. "I still hate myself for it."

He takes my shoulders, pulling me away so he can look me in the eye. "You didn't kill anyone, Minny."

"But I tried."

"We did nothing wrong, unless living is a crime."

I take a shaky breath and release it slowly. "I don't want to be a killer, Eli."

He smiles gently at me. "Then don't be. Be a survivor."

Despite my tangled emotions, a laugh bursts out of me. "That's so cheesy."

He chuckles. "Yeah, but you're smiling again."

"I'm sorry I interrupted your date." Not really, but I should be.

"It's fine. I'll catch up with her tomorrow. I need sleep anyhow."

I look around, reluctant to return to my room and thoughts. "Do you mind if I crash in here?"

He shrugs. "Pick a bed, any bed." I smile and roll into the one across the room from where Sierra had been sitting.

"Eli?"

"Yeah?"

"Would you really have shot Tony this morning?"

There's a long pause. "Honestly, I'm not sure there's anything I wouldn't do to keep you safe." His answer is so close to how my father had described his own desire to keep me safe. No matter what my father's fears were, I can't bring myself to distrust Eli in any way. Even in his werewolf form, he stood beside me. In my gut, I know I am safe with him no matter what lies ahead.

Tears prick the corners of my eyes again, and I struggle to control them. My emotions have seriously been like a roller coaster over the last two days. "Thank you," I finally say. The answering silence tells me he's already asleep.

CHAPTER 6

Without any sunlight to brighten the room, it feels almost impossible for me to wake up the next morning. I manage to drag myself out of bed, only to find that Eli's already gone. I check the time on my phone. It's still early, only six. I dress quickly and head to the cafeteria.

Eli is with Sierra, enjoying some bacon with his eggs today. I help myself to some breakfast and join them. Sierra gives me the cold shoulder, literally snubbing me.

I clear my throat awkwardly. "I owe you an apology," I tell her. "I was having a bit of a panic attack. I shouldn't have interrupted you like that, and I'm sorry."

She's quiet for a moment as she pushes her eggs around her plate. She sighs. "Alright, apology accepted." Then she smiles flirtatiously at Elias. "I remember right where we left off."

I try not to choke in disgust at that comment. At that moment, a guy maybe a year or so older than us, walks in. He has sandy brown hair and blue eyes. A scar runs down his face from the left side, across his right eye, and along his jawline. His gait is confident and predatorial. The sight of him draws all of my attention. If he's not a werewolf, then I don't know what is.

"Are there many werewolves that work here?" I ask Sierra.

She wrinkles her nose in disgust. "Eww, gross, of course not. We hunt werewolves. Why would we *work* with them?"

"No reason," I mumble at my plate, exchanging a look with Eli. Tony breaks the awkward moment, sliding in beside us with his tray. I'd been so focused on the other guy, filling his tray with various proteins, I hadn't even noticed Tony come in.

"Hey guys, how'd you sleep?" he asks.

"Like the dead," Eli answers. "Minny didn't so much as flinch when I left the room."

Sierra frowns. "Why would she? She was in an entirely different room."

Eli shakes his head and shovels more food into his mouth. "Nah, she was having trouble sleeping, so she crashed on the extra bunk in my room."

"It's not weird sharing a room with a girl like that?" She asks. I'm quietly enjoying the bit of jealousy she's experiencing.

He shrugs. "After bathing together when we were little, pretty much nothing is weird between us anymore." It's true. One time, he walked in on me while I was changing, and it wasn't any more awkward than if a family member had done it. I yelled at him like he was some pesky brother and he giggled as he retreated. I have to refrain from smiling at the pout on Sierra's face as she pushes her food around dejectedly.

Tony seems to have bypassed the entire detour from his original question. "That's great! I'm glad you slept well."

"Tony, who's that?" I ask, switching gears as I nod in the direction of the guy/werewolf now making his way along the buffet table.

His smile disappears as soon as he follows my line of vision. "Zev Devante Lycidas. He's a crazy mofo. My advice, steer clear of him."

"That seems unkind." I watch as people clear a path for him like he's diseased or something. A couple actually stumble in their haste to get away.

"Trust me, you don't want to get in his way," Tony reassures me.

"Oh, I'd like to get in his way just once," Sierra says dreamily. All three of us stare at her in surprise. "What?" She demands. "On a scale of one to ten, he's clearly a six. Plus, I bet he's an animal between the sheets."

"Really? I would have put him at an eight, at least," I tell her, tilting my head slightly as I watch Zev exit the room.

She shrugs. "Maybe, but he's got that scar. It costs him points in my opinion." I wonder how many points his lineage would cost him if she knew it.

Elias swallows the last of his food. "You guys are great for my ego, you know." he says drily.

I smile broadly and pat his cheek. "Cheer up, good buddy. You're definitely no less than a five."

Sierra giggles and grasps his arm. "An even ten in my book."

I roll my eyes and pick up my dishes. "We should do some training today. Dad and Dorris would have our hides for missing the last two days." I swallow hard at the way those words hit me, even as they come out of my mouth. Like being hit in the gut with the reminder of their deaths.

The others follow Eli and me to the training room. Tony grumbles about his own number on our scale. I don't want to hurt his feelings, but I'd maybe give him a four or five if I was being generous. While he's well built, he has rather small hands. His eyes are just slightly too far apart and his nose sort of wanders to the left.

In the training room, I choose a crossbow for the shooting range. It's one of my favorite weapons and one I'm least versed in. I'm testing its weight when a voice startles me.

"Hey." It's more of a growl than an actual word.

I spin on my heel to find myself face-to-face with Zev. Up close, I notice his scarred eye is the cloudy blue that indicates blindness. "Damn, man. You should really wear a bell or something."

He ignores my comment. "That's mine," he says in that same growling voice.

"Are you sure? Because it was on the wall for general use."

Now he really does growl. A sound that usually cows me when Elias does it, but without my parents or Dorris to back me and after the week I've had, it just pushes my buttons. I glare up at him. He's roughly a head taller than me. "Don't growl at me! If you don't want people using your weapons, then don't leave them on the public wall."

He matches my glare with one of his own as he stalks closer. My legs want to back down, but my pride won't let me. Eli appears at my side then. "Is there a problem here?"

Neither of us responds, but I notice Zev's eyes grow darker. His actions up to now were merely for intimidation, I realize, with no real malice behind them. But Eli's mere presence seems to crawl right under his skin. I don't think two male werewolves in such close proximity is a good idea.

Zev reaches out his arm and my muscles coil instinctively. I can feel Elias tense beside me, ready to lunge. Zev takes a second, smaller crossbow off the wall. Plucking the one I'm holding out of my hands, he replaces it with the new one before taking down the bolts for his. He doesn't even go around us, just pushes between us like we're not standing right here.

We turn to watch him stalk away, people scrambling out of his way once more. "That guy reeks of werewolf. Like, pure-blood werewolf," Eli says.

I snort. "No kidding. Not to mention his name might as well be Wolfie McWolfington." He gives me a quizzical look. "Zev Lycidas? It means Wolf Wolfson."

"Huh, way to label a guy,"

I smirk at him. "Because your name is so much better?"

"Wolfric means wolf power. It doesn't directly translate to wolf," he says defensively.

"What the hell was that?" Tony demands, appearing out of the group of people. "Didn't I *just* tell you, not even ten minutes ago, to stay out of his way? Are you trying to get yourselves killed?"

I shrug. "It's fine. I just had the wrong crossbow."

Tony starts to argue further, but Eli interrupts him. "If he's such a threat, why is he allowed to stay?"

"Langley brought him in years ago. He taught him everything he knows. He refuses to see how Zev is a threat and insists he stay. Being he's one of our top hunters, Benjamin has let him keep Zev around."

Elias takes the crossbow from me and hangs it up. "We need to talk," he says suddenly, grabbing my hand to drag me away.

"I guess we'll catch you later," I call over my shoulder to Tony, trying not to trip.

Eli leads me back to his room, closing and locking the door behind us. "Remember that shirt I told you about? The one that smelled like my father?" I nod. "Langley smells just like that."

My eyes widen at the revelation. "You think Langley might..."

He rubs a hand through his hair. "I don't know, maybe. But that would make him a werewolf and Sierra says they don't employ werewolves here."

"At least not knowingly," I point out.

He nods. "Exactly, which brings me to another thought. What if Langley's a spy and he brought Zev here as his right hand? What if they're learning all the hunters' secrets and reporting to the local werewolves? I mean, Langley seems pretty high in ranking here. He's got to be learning all sorts of things."

"Sure, I suppose that's a possibility, or maybe he's just some guy who wears the same cologne as your father. Maybe he doesn't even know what Zev is."

He's shaking his head. "No, it's a very specific scent, natural, not cologne."

"Does he smell like a werewolf?"

Another shake. "No, but... what if it's easier to hide the scent as we get older?"

"Why would he need to? Hunters don't have the same sense of smell as werewolves."

"But you knew what Zev was before you even knew his name. Before I confirmed it for you. I saw it in your eyes."

"I didn't *smell* him, though. I just... sensed it."

"Look, Langley seems to have been close to our parents. Is it possible your mom just happened to have one of his shirts somehow and just told you it was your father's so you could feel close to him?"

He lets out a long sigh. "Yeah, I guess, but that scent is the only lead I had." He sinks onto the bed dejectedly. "How am I supposed to find him now?"

"We could still ask Langley. Even if he's not your father, he may know who is."

"Ok, let's try that, I guess." He rises and leads the way out of the room.

"Wait, we're going now?"

"Well, yeah. It's why we're here, isn't it? They said they would help us."

They never actually said that, just pointed out that we were unprepared, but it is why we're here. I suppose now is as good a time as any to find out what they know.

Langley has a small office space in the corridor leading to Benjamin's office. Lucky for us, he's sitting at his desk when we get there. He's propped his door open for people to come and go. He looks up when we enter and smiles. "Ah, what a nice surprise. I trust you two are settling in well?"

"Yes, thank you," I reply.

"We have some questions to ask you, though," Elias says.

Langley's smile fades to concern. "Of course, please, come in." Eli shuts the door behind us, and we take a seat.

"You were close to my mother, correct?" He asks.

"Yes," Langley answers. "Professionally speaking."

"Do you know if she was seeing anyone before I was born?"

A shadow crosses his eyes, something he attempts to hide by looking down at his paperwork. "No." He takes a deep breath. "I'm sorry, Elias. I can't tell you who your father is."

Eli fidgets a little. "Ok, it's just that Mom used to have this shirt she would wrap me in, and she said it was my father's, but it... it had your name on the tag." I guess that's one way to put it.

Something sparks in Langley's eyes, like he's pleased. "She must have been mistaken. I have no children."

I can see the hurt in Eli's eyes. Even without him saying it, I can tell he feels like his father is rejecting him. "So, you loved her but she wasn't interested?" I ask, hoping to strike a nerve.

Langley's gaze snaps to me so fast I know I must have succeeded. "I don't know what you're talking about."

I smile sweetly. "Eyes tend not to lie, sir. Don't feel bad. We've all been there before."

He sighs. "Fine, if you must know, I pursued Dorris for quite some time, but nothing ever came of it. Then she simply disappeared one day. I never heard from her or your parents again. I swear, that's all I can tell you. I'm sorry I can't be of more use to you."

Now Eli sighs. "It's fine. Thanks anyway."

We exit the office just as Zev reaches the door. He scowls at us, shoulders by, and shuts the door in our faces. "Nice guy," Eli mutters.

"Maybe he's having a bad day," I offer. "I did touch his crossbow, after all."

Eli chuckles. "Yeah, I'm sure that ruined his whole day." We step out of the doorway but linger near the office.

"What are you doing?" I ask.

"Shh," he whispers. I listen, but it's just muffled voices. After several minutes, he grabs my hand and dashes for the training room. As soon as he stops, I ask him what he heard. "Nothing useful. Langley was just checking in on him."

"Then why'd we run?"

"Because they were finishing up, and I didn't want to get caught eavesdropping."

I had been excited about practicing with the crossbow, but I have too many other questions bubbling in my mind. Do other hunters sense werewolves? Are werewolf packs similar to wolf packs in their hierarchy? What exactly are hunters, anyway? I had thought to ask Eli about some of the werewolf questions, but he's lived his entire life around hunters so there's a lot he doesn't know about werewolves.

"Do you think there's a library around here?" I ask Elias.

He shrugs. "Probably. The place is big enough."

Luckily, Sierra is still in the training room and agrees to show me where the library is. It's done with a roll of her eyes, but at least she's willing to take us there.

Once I start my research, I find myself getting sucked in and the rest of the day flies past without my notice. I learn how hunters are their own being set apart from humans, yet still human. There's a book with images depicting the hierarchy of werewolves. It is indeed very similar to normal wolves.

One book is entirely dedicated to debunking myths about werewolves. They can shift at any time, not just the full moon. It's a conscious motion for them, like lifting an arm. Generally, they remain conscious of who they are as well and keep much of their human brain while shifted. There have been some recorded cases, however, where the werewolf decided to stay in wolf form and eventually succumbed to the animal part of their brain.

And silver isn't the only thing that can kill them. In fact, it's considered too strong for proper bullets. A werewolf can be killed in much the same ways as any human. I already knew this from experience, but it's still interesting to learn about the bullets.

What really sucks me in, though, is reading about the alphas. There's a strict set of rules for how an alpha is chosen. Most of them are born to it, inheriting the position from their father before them. Sometimes an alpha is killed, and the title passes to the one who killed them. Rarely, like once every two hundred years or so, someone comes along who rises to the rank of alpha through sheer force of will alone. These ones are called true alphas and they are the strongest of the werewolves.

I'd never heard of this before. Not in any of the stories my dad used to tell me or any of the books I've read in the past. I wonder if a half-blood werewolf could become a true alpha? Eli certainly has plenty of will-power.

Eli left me in order to practice in the training room. He's not much of a book-worm so he would have been incredibly bored if he stayed with me. I was reluctant to let him go, still feeling uncertain in this new place and clinging to the one familiar thing I have. I couldn't justify keeping him somewhere he'd be bored to tears, so I didn't ask him to stay.

Eventually, Eli comes to check on me and I notice Sierra is still following him. He seems to be attempting to put some space between them. I assume it's because of her disgust over werewolves. I'm sure it's hard to be interested in someone who can make your entire species sound like slugs.

When I finish in the library, I head to the training room to find Eli so we can get some supper. It's not hard to locate him. I assume because I find him predictable. I've always just sort of known where to find him most days.

Tony sits with us again at supper. I'm starting to wonder if he has any other friends. He informs us that John and Langley are working on a plan to find Eli's father.

I wonder how they plan on doing that if they don't even know who he is, but I guess they have their resources. Eli's pissed that they didn't tell us this sooner. I'm just glad things are moving forward. We'll hear more about it tomorrow, according to Tony.

CHAPTER 7

Assuming either John or Langley will summon us when they're ready, Elias and I hit the training room again the next day. Until we're given a directive, there isn't much else to do around here. He challenges me to a match and Tony proclaims he will fight the winner.

Eli's a difficult opponent. We've been training together for so long we know exactly what to expect from each other. By sheer luck, I pin him on his back. Tony steps up and gives his staff a twirl as I shake out my hands. The cuts are starting to heal, but still tender. Tony smirks, clearly feeling cocky. It isn't luck that plants him on his ass. More like his own overconfidence.

Eli steps forward for another go but is halted by a girl who steps forward first. "If it's ok, I'd like to try," she says. She's small, roughly my height, with long, black curls and deep brown eyes. With her pretty features, she could be a model.

Eli gives me a questioning look and I shrug my answer. The more variation I get, the better. He steps aside with a bow and fancy hand flourish. The girl giggles, revealing a perfect set of dimples.

"Thank you!" She steps forward and offers me a handshake. "My name is Kalia, but my friends call me Kali."

I shake her hand. "Amane, Elias calls me Minny." I incline my head towards Eli.

We step apart and take our stances. She's good, very well-trained, but she's also hesitant. She seems afraid of hurting me. I give a few jabs to sort of test her. She deflects but makes no attempt at launching her own attack.

I pick up the pace a bit more and she matches my pace. Finally, she makes a sweep at my legs but doesn't put any real force behind it, so it doesn't hurt, let alone knock me off my feet.

Her next swing hits my ribs. It stings some, but still feels gentle even for a practice match. In the end, her caution costs her the match. I make a feint towards her left and swing back to her right, dropping low to sweep her feet and then I am over her with my staff at her heart.

Eli steps forward to help her up. "That was a good match," he tells her encouragingly.

She flashes her dimples and turns to face me. "Thank you, Amane, that was fun."

I open my mouth to answer, but the guy stalking up behind her stops my words. Zev steps up and takes her staff before she realizes what's happening. The crowd that's gathered sucks in a breath as one. Over the last two days, I've noticed crowds are normal around matches like this. Until now, I've done my best to ignore the onlookers.

"My turn," Zev says in a flat tone. Kalia dips her head shyly and scurries away before I can thank her for the match. Eli puffs himself up, ready to get between Zev and me, but I stop him with a quick shake of my head. He takes a place in the crowd with Tony and Kalia, his eyes flashing daggers, every muscle remaining tensed.

I swallow hard and take my stance. Zev stands perfectly still, his eyes pinned on me. For a moment we're motionless, then my nerves take hold and I move to strike. I know better than to leap in like this, But I just need one of us to move.

My attack is sloppy. Too wide with my weight distributed all wrong. It's simple for him to step aside and let me hurtle by. I flush with embarrassment as I regain my balance. Taking a deep breath, I turn to face him once more. I exhale slowly, settling into my center before moving to engage him once more. This time I've got it right. I can feel it in my stance and the way my staff feels like an extension of me.

He has me down in three quick moves, faster than a striking snake. My mind is left spinning as I hit the floor, trying to figure out how this happened so fast. I get the sense he could have had me down in one but was giving me some type of chance.

He comes to stand over me. "Langley wants you, Tony, and the ass in his office," he tells me, and then just walks away.

Eli and I exchange hopeful looks before following him. Maybe Langley has decided to help.

The door is open. John is sitting in the extra chair while Zev lounges against the wall. Langley sits behind his desk expectantly. We file in and wait for him to speak. Zev glances at Eli, who is almost brushing shoulders with him. He glares and knocks Eli sideways with a shove on the shoulder. "There's not a whole lot of room left here!" Eli snaps.

"Then make some," Zev growls back. Tony edges away from them until he is pressing against my shoulder.

"Boys," Langley speaks up. "Save the squabbling for later." His voice is stern, but that amused look is back in his eyes.

They glare at each other another moment before breaking eye contact. Actively ignoring each other, they fold their arms over their chests in similar stances of forced indifference. "Now, Elias," Langley begins. "You were planning on heading into the mountains to find your father, correct?"

"Yeah, but my only lead was that shirt and clearly that was a dead end. It's hard to find someone if you don't know who you're looking for."

"I wouldn't think of it as a dead end so much as a helpful suggestion. It lead you to us, after all, and John and I have an idea of where we might begin looking."

Eli narrows his eyes at Langley. "Then you *do* know who he is. You lied to us."

"Aren't you a bit old to be crying for Daddy?" Zev asks before Langley can respond.

Elias turns his glare back on him. "When you lose the family you know, you tend to look for what's left."

Something dark, almost sad, flashes across Zev's eyes, but Langley's speaking before he can respond. "That's enough! You two are going to have to get along. We're all going on this mission. Together."

"We don't need him," Eli shoots back.

"Good, I didn't want to go," Zev pushes past Eli to leave.

Langley stands and plants both his hands on his desk, storm clouds replacing the previous humor in his eyes. His voice is a low warning. "Get your ass back in this room."

Zev freezes in the doorway. I don't think anyone in their right mind would go against Langley's orders while he's using that tone. Taking a deep breath, Zev turns around, but doesn't come back into the room. He meets Langley's eyes evenly. "I apologize for my behavior, sir. It will not happen again."

Tony's jaw drops. Zev's eyes hold nothing but sincerity.

With just his tone, Langley had brought a pure-blood werewolf to heel. It speaks volumes about their relationship and the level of respect Zev must have for him.

Langley softens a bit. "Can you please, at the very least, ignore each other unless it's vital to communicate? You don't have to like each other, just be able to work together."

Zev nods. "Yes, sir."

Langley looks at Eli. "Elias?"

Eli fidgets, grumbles, and finally sighs. He meets Langley's eyes. "Yes, sir."

Langley smiles in triumph and returns to his seat. "Excellent! Ok then, John, thoughts? We have six in our party. Should we include any others?"

John considers for a moment while his eyes rove over each of us, taking our measure. "Perhaps Amane would like an additional female companion."

All eyes turn to me. I shrug, trying to ignore the blush creeping up my neck. "Doesn't matter to me, as long as Sierra's not coming."

Tony frowns. "What's wrong with Sierra?"

"Her passionate dislike for werewolves, for one thing." Not to mention the way she hangs off Eli.

John looks confused. "Most hunters don't like werewolves. They're vicious beasts, it's why we hunt them. You, of all people, should know this." Eli and Zev both shift uncomfortably.

"I mean, sure, they didn't make a great first impression." An understatement. "But they can't all be murderous beings."

Tony snorts derisively. "That's all they do is murder."

I narrow my eyes at him and cross my arms over my chest. "Really, Tony? Have you met every werewolf?"

He looks sheepish, as his eyes dart to John and Langley in a vain hope of backup. "Well, no, but…"

"Then shut up," I tell him.

Langley holds up his hands to silence us. "That's enough. While Amane's opinion is not the most popular around here, it's her right to have it. Amane, if not Sierra, is there another girl you want to join us?"

I shrug again. "If I must pick one, I guess I'd pick Kalia. She's the only other one I've spent any amount of time with."

Langley nods his head. "Alright then, Zev, could you let Kalia know she is needed for this mission? Tell her to be ready to head out at six a.m. tomorrow." Zev nods and leaves. The rest of us are dismissed to prepare and rest.

CHAPTER 8

Kalia's practically bubbling over with excitement when we meet her at the front entrance the next day. "Good morning! Are you guys on the mission too? This is my first one, ever. I could barely believe it when Zev told me."

She pauses and frowns slightly. "Though, to be honest, I couldn't believe he was talking to me at all. He doesn't speak to anyone except Langley usually, unless he absolutely has to." Now she gets a distracted look. "Plus, I was too nervous to grasp what he was saying until he was walking away. He is one scary dude."

She stops with a look of shock. "Oh, that was rude of me. Don't tell him I said that. It's just... he has a reputation. And he moves just like a predator. Like he's hunting you. It's kind of terrifying."

Tony joins us then, cutting into her rambling. "Talking the noobies' ears off already, Kali?"

A look of horror covers her face. "I am so sorry! I don't usually talk this much. I just tend to babble when I'm excited."

Zev joins us next and Kalia pales, her babbling comes to an abrupt halt. Tony shifts slightly, so he's almost behind me. As though I'd be any form of protection against Zev. Zev's eyes move between Eli and me, ignoring our cowering friends.

"No weapons?" He asks. He has his crossbow across his back along with a gun and dagger on his belt. Even Kalia has a gun. Tony has three, two handguns and a rifle that is slung across his back.

"We're armed, just not visibly," Eli answers defiantly.

Zev ignores him and meets my gaze. "Anything on the weapons rack is fair game for missions."

"Really?" I ask excitedly. My mind immediately jumps to the crossbow. He nods and I drop my backpack at Eli's feet. "Watch my stuff."

I run off so fast I just barely catch his retort. "Unless it sprouts legs, I doubt it's going anywhere."

By the time I get back, Langley has arrived. "Here, I got you this." I pass a short sword to Elias.

He sucks in his breath as I hand him a Norman sword. He takes it reverently, feeling its heft and balance. "I can take this?" He asks Langley softly.

Langley smiles at the childlike rapture on his face. "As long as you know how to use it and don't stab any of us with it."

Eli beams at me. "Awesome!" Dorris started sword training with us when we were around eight. It's always been Eli's favorite weapon, but he's never held one quite as nice as this one.

My father had some, but they weren't for training. They were family heirlooms, two katanas and a wakizashi. Eventually, they would have been passed down to me, but they're probably buried under the rubble of my home now. Had I not been so deeply in shock, I would have thought to grab them before Eli set the house on fire.

"Alright kiddos, John is waiting for us up top with the van." Langley announces, pulling me back up from my dark thoughts. He herds us into the elevator.

The ride up is just as unnerving as the ride down had been. This time it's Zev that grunts, "steady." at me when my hand reaches for stability. For half a second I consider taking my hand back, but he doesn't seem to mind it and I'm pretty sure I'll fall if I let go. In the end, I'm glad I kept my hand on him. Especially when we jerk to a stop, I have to fist my hand in his shirt to avoid slamming into the wall. His muscles tense as he supports our combined weight.

"Isn't there another way in and out?" I ask as the door slides open.

Langley grins, looking back before stepping out. "Yes, but this one's more fun."

Zev glances at where my hand still clutches a handful of his shirt and then meets my eyes. I release him quickly. "Sorry," I mutter, blushing.

We can tell through the van's tinted windows that there's already a passenger waiting inside. We slide the door open to find Sierra in the back seat. Eli looks somewhere between shocked and disappointed. Tony has a smirk on his face, like he's somehow won. Zev just looks pissed.

"I thought our team stopped at seven," Langley comments.

Kalia gasps. Her hand flies to her mouth. "I'm sorry! I just thought... We've done all our training as a team. So, I thought we could be partners. I'm sorry!"

All the men's eyes are on me again. They're making me decide. I assume it's because I was so adamant about Sierra not coming in the first place. I sigh to myself. Both Eli and Zev's eyes are drilling a hole through me, but I can't reasonably send her away. Forcing a smile, I pat Kalia's shoulder. "It's fine. Strength in numbers, right?"

She smiles in relief. I climb past her to take a seat beside Sierra. It's better that I'm beside her than Eli or Zev. If she starts spewing hate about werewolves again, I wouldn't put it past Zev to strangle her.

I drop my gear over the seat, into the back, and then strap in. Kalia follows suit while the guys pile their gear into the trunk using the back hatch. The younger men pile into the row in front of us. Langley takes shotgun. Then we're off.

Somehow, we're headed deeper into the mountains. I had thought we were at the end of the road, yet here we are, driving further. I let my mind wander until I become stumped on a thought. Something I'd been unable to discover in the library.

I sensed Zev was a werewolf, a notion that was confirmed when Eli smelled him, but I already knew it in my bones. Shouldn't the other hunters be able to sense this? If they could, I can guarantee neither Tony, nor Sierra would be here right now. Also, Sierra wouldn't be so interested in Eli.

Even now she's leaning forward to whisper in his ear. I can see by his expression that he's trying to be patient. I'd like to elbow her in the ribs, if for no other reason than to make her sit still, but, like Eli, I do my best to reign in my temper.

Just when I'm about to snap, we roll to a stop. "It's all on foot from here, guys." Langley announces. Eli and I simultaneously breathe a sigh of relief. At least outdoors, we can put some space between us and Sierra.

"Isn't it suspicious, just leaving the van here?" I ask.

"No one comes this far," John answers. "Even planes rarely come this way."

"Ok." I'm not convinced, but he knows the area better than I do.

"What exactly is the objective of this mission?" Sierra asks. Kalia gives her a look of surprise when she realizes she missed a vital bit of information when taking a mission. In all her excitement, she'd forgotten to ask for herself. Or maybe she was too intimidated by Zev to ask.

"Finding Eli's father," Tony answers.

Sierra looks confused. "And you expect to find him in the mountains?"

Tony shrugs. "I guess so. We're all just following Langley and John." She looks between the men with a bewildered expression before shaking her head. The questionability of their plan isn't lost on any of us, but none of us will speak against Langley.

We fall in behind the two men and begin our hike. Elias walks beside Kalia just behind our fearless leaders. Again, I'm forced to push my jealousy down where no one will ever see it. Sierra and Tony are next, with me behind them. I glance back to make sure Zev is behind me only to find him staring into space, a look of disappointment and anguish on his face.

"Zev?" I call back. He seems to shake himself before bringing his focus to me. "Are you coming?" He glances off through the trees once more before moving to catch up, his hardened mask falling back over his face. That was strange.

"I question the sanity of wandering into werewolf infested mountains with only a group of kids to back you," Sierra announces loudly.

"Tony and Zev have both proven themselves many times in the field, and Amane and Elias were raised and trained by some of our best," John calls back. "That's a pretty solid team, in my opinion." He's putting quite a bit of stock in our abilities. Not that I'm not flattered, I just think he's expecting more than we can give.

Despite Tony's warnings of Zev's potential for being dangerous, I feel more secure knowing he's behind me. Having a werewolf back you is rather comforting when you're headed through werewolf territory. That sense of security only increases when Langley drops back to join him.

I may talk big, but, truthfully, strange werewolves scare the shit out of me. I still have flashbacks to the terror of that last night at home when I'm alone in the dark. Eli's been kind enough to let me stay in his room since that first night at Hunters' Headquarters.

I'm grateful now for the extensive hikes my dad used to take us on since the time we started walking. He called them 'nature hikes', but they were rather intense for something meant to be enjoyable. I always wondered why we couldn't walk at a more leisurely pace, or rest more often. Dad's answer was that 'nature waits for no one'. It didn't make sense at the time, but now I realize it was all part of our training to build endurance. Because of those 'nature hikes', I'm able to keep up today while also carrying all of my gear. A feat that both Sierra and Kalia are struggling with.

We stop twice for them to rest before Eli and Zev take their gear and add it to their own so the girls can walk unencumbered. The second time Sierra sat down, Zev growled in frustration, snatched up her bag, and just kept walking. That's when Eli offered to take Kalia's, since she was also struggling and falling behind. Whether he was being chivalrous, or just competitive, I'm not sure.

Now, I'm the one in the back and I'm not enjoying it in the least. Eli drops back to walk with me, bringing with him a wash of relief and a silly flutter in my stomach. "How are you holding up?" He asks.

"Fine, just a little anxious being at the back," I answer honestly.

"How come?" He looks concerned and glances over his shoulder as though he might find us being followed.

I take my time answering, feeling somewhat embarrassed about it. "I keep having nightmares about that night, when that one came through the window and grabbed me... It just has me on edge out here. I keep looking back."

"Yeah, I can't shake that night either," he admits, his voice heavy. "I thought I'd lost you for a minute." He smiles. "But we're here now, and still in one piece. Just trust your instincts to know if something's really wrong and remember, we're not alone anymore. We've got trained hunters to watch our backs."

I return his smile, even if I'm not feeling it. I nod my agreement. Those 'trained hunters' are a contributing factor to my anxiety. Suppose one of them realizes Eli has werewolf blood in his veins. What's stopping them from killing him?

We stop to eat not long after this conversation. It's a quick, light meal of jerky and crusty bread, food that will hold well without refrigeration. To my relief, Zev takes the rear once more, remaining there for the rest of the day.

Conversation is light and kept just above a whisper. For some reason, we all seem afraid to offend the surrounding forest with excess noise. Overhead, Spring birds fill in the silence with their cheerful songs as they flit between barely budding branches.

CHAPTER 9

The temperature drops with the sun. By the time we stop to make camp, it feels like it's twenty degrees Fahrenheit. We drop our packs and Zev and Elias both sniff the air before declaring that snow is coming. It's as though they rehearsed it, they're so in sync with this proclamation. I struggle to smother a laugh as they glare at each other.

"I'm going hunting," Zev growls.

"Don't go far," Langley warns. Zev doesn't respond, disappearing back into the trees. Langley smiles at the group. "At least we'll eat well tonight." I guess he has good faith in Zev's hunting abilities.

By the time he returns with a couple of rabbits, the sun is completely down and we're all huddled around a toasty fire. I had questioned the logic of starting a fire where werewolves might see us, but Langley pointed out they'd smell us either way. Plus, we can't be expected to eat Zev's catch raw.

Langley helps to skin and gut the rabbits, a process that causes Sierra to gag theatrically. I have no doubt in my mind that this is the exact reason Zev decided to sit beside her while he worked. Kalia does her best to simply avert her eyes. I think Kalia is too tender-hearted for such activities. She's one of those super sweet people who just can't handle when a life is snuffed out. I think she missed the memo that, as hunters, that's what we do. Snuff out lives.

Still, I take pity on her and suggest she help me roll out bedrolls for later. She jumps on the chance to do something other than watch the rabbits be prepped. She chats to me about the evening air or anything else that comes to mind as well, further distracting herself.

We're all munching on rabbit, except Tony, who's eating dried fruit, when a chill runs down my spine like an icy finger. I stop mid-bite and notice Zev and Elias have also paused. No one else seems to notice. Another chill followed by hair-raising goose-bumps run over my body and all three of us are on our feet, weapons at the ready. The others have stopped eating to ask what's happening. Langley skips the questioning, joining us on his feet with a gun in hand.

I notice a flash in the trees and track it with my crossbow. A moment later, a werewolf leaps out of the woods, straight for Zev. Kalia and Sierra scream while John and Tony jump to their feet and draw their guns.

The werewolf rushes in, too fast for Zev to get a shot, and he's forced to dodge to the side. It skids to a stop just short of the fire. The werewolf doubles back, only to find my crossbow bolt buried in its chest.

Another werewolf flies out of the trees to be shot by Tony before it's three steps into the camp. A third follows, coming for me this time. Now it's my turn to dodge, just before Eli puts a bullet in it.

My heart's hammering from the rush of adrenaline, but I don't sense anymore werewolves nearby. I survey the fallen, and it settles into my mind what I've just done. My entire body starts shaking so hard my teeth chatter. My crossbow slips out of my hands and lands on the ground as I sink to my knees.

Eli's at my side in an instant. "Minny? Minny, look at me." I can't pull my eyes off the werewolf I killed. From somewhere far off I hear voices asking if I'm alright or injured.

"Amane," Eli's voice presses. Still, I'm frozen. "Ichinose!" That brings my eyes sliding slowly to him simply by instinct. He doesn't use my last name unless the situation is dire.

He takes my face between his hands so I can't look away. "You did what had to be done. Us or them."

"They were people too." I manage to whisper before the tears slip out.

"Us or them, Amane," he repeats in a gentle voice.

Langley squats beside him and takes my hand. "Amane, he was planning to kill Zev. You had a shot, and you took it. Sometimes that's all you can do."

I nod through my sob. It was a bad werewolf, not like Elias and Zev. "You protected your teammates, and that's a good thing," Langley continues. I try to pull myself together. Now who missed the memo on a hunter's job?

My tears come to a stuttering halt. Kalia gives me an uncertain hug and leads me back to the fire. Eli presses a water canteen into my hand to drink from. I've finally composed myself for the most part, as long as I don't look at the three dead werewolves.

"I don't see what the big deal is," Sierra says, as loudly as she states any of her opinions. "They're just filthy, mindless beasts." And just like that, my temper snaps. My fist collides with her face before I realize it's swinging. Every time they talk shit about werewolves, I take it as a personal affront on Elias. It pisses me off. How dare they say those things about him?

She falls backward with a grunt. Blood seeps between the fingers she has clamped over her nose. "What the Hell? You little bitch!" She shrieks. "I think you broke my nose! Over werewolves?"

"I pray to my ancestors you choke on your own poison one day, Sierra," I tell her, my rage still hot in my chest.

Everyone else is sitting in shock until Eli speaks up. "Well, at least she's not crying anymore." John and Tony finally react, scrambling to find something to stop the bleeding. If I didn't know any better, I'd swear Zev and Langley just exchanged smirks.

Guard duty is split into four groups. I'm on second shift with John. Zev and Langley have first shift. There are two reasons for the division of our shifts. One, Zev and Eli would probably kill each other if they shared a shift. Two, it ensures Sierra and Kalia are partnered with people who are ready to react. They didn't make an outstanding impression during the werewolf attack.

The first snowflakes start to fall as Zev nudges me awake. He'll be taking up occupation in my bedroll while I'm on duty. We only laid out six bedrolls since only six of us will be sleeping at a time.

It also has the added benefit that after the first shift, no one has to climb into cold bedding. Plus, less packing in the morning.

There's a hush that comes with the falling snow. Even the air has no desire to shake the trees for fear of making a sound. John and I sit on opposite ends of the camp. When we start to doze, we get up and do a quick sweep of the perimeter to get our blood moving. Someone was kind enough to remove the werewolves' bodies, so we don't have to worry about tripping on those, and I don't have to look at what I've done again.

It feels like an eternity before I finally get to wake Eli and roll into his warmed bedroll. I'm sound asleep in seconds. The next thing I know, Tony's shaking me awake to the start of a new day. As dangerous as Tony claims Zev is, he's a hell of a lot gentler about waking a person than Tony.

"I'm sleeping, not dead. You don't have to shake me so hard." I grumble at him as I sit up, a layer of snow tumbling off the bedding and dropping from my hair.

He smiles apologetically. "Sorry, I'm used to having to wake John. He might as well be dead when he sleeps."

Sierra's attempting to wake Eli with gentle nudges on the other side of camp and I give Tony a wry smile. "Yeah, I can relate." Climbing to my feet, I go to her aid. A lifetime of experience has taught me that the way to wake Eli is to remove any semblance of comfort. I unzip his sleeping bag and tug hard until he rolls out onto the cold, snow covered ground.

He sits up and looks around. "What the… hey!" He scowls at me as I shake out the bedroll and roll it up into a tight bundle.

"Morning, sunshine," I answer with an innocent smile. By now the rest of our little camp is awake and bustling to pack up. Zev is nowhere to be seen, a fact Elias notices instantly and begins grumbling about. He feels Zev is shirking his duties.

Not long after everything is packed, he returns. "How was scouting?" Langley asks in a tone that's clearly meant to shut Eli up. It works well.

Dorris and Langley have a lot in common in this aspect. They're both intense people with tight grips on their emotions. They've had to be. Lesser people would never be able to raise werewolves.

"It looks clear ahead. I didn't find any signs of other werewolves in the area," Zev reports.

Langley nods. "Good. With any luck, those three were on their own out here."

Before long we're trudging up the mountain side again, munching nuts and dried fruit for breakfast. Zev takes the rear again. It makes me wonder if he overheard my conversation with Eli the day before, or if he just prefers being in the back. Either way, it helps quiet my nerves so I can focus more clearly on my gut instincts.

Up ahead, Kalia and Eli are talking and laughing amiably. They've gotten close really fast. I like Kalia, I really do. She's ridiculously sweet and kind, which sort of interferes with her ability to defend herself because she's so reluctant to hurt anyone. I'm also incredibly jealous of her right now, which adds fuel to my hiking energy, but also makes me hate her a little.

It's not the usual jealousy I get when Eli flirts with other girls, though. It's less about him apparently not seeing me as a girl, and more about missing my best friend. In two days, we've spoken all of twice, and one of those times was because I was hysterical over taking a life. Of course, I'm not going to be like, 'hey, pay attention to me', so I just rage quietly. Allowing my emotions to propel me up the mountain.

"Where exactly are we headed?" Sierra asks almost two hours later. She's been complaining about her legs and face hurting all morning. In her defense, the blow to her nose did leave her with two black eyes. No, I do not feel one bit of remorse for my actions.

"There's a cave just over the mountain," Langley answers. "About another day and a half."

That doesn't make any sense to me. It takes eight people to scope out a cave? And what would give John and Langley any reason to believe Eli's father would be there, unless they know more than they're telling us?

"Why would Eli's father be in a cave on top of a mountain?" Sierra demands.

"He's probably not, but we may find a lead as to who, or where he could be," John explains.

"In a cave? On top of a mountain?" Sierra repeats pointedly. I agree, it seems sketchy. At least, it would, from the view of someone who believes Elias is all hunter. It makes perfect sense if you know his father is a werewolf.

"Am I the only one wondering how this is Hunter's business?" Tony asks.

"It's not," Langley replies. "It's personal. Dorris and the Ichinoses were close friends of mine. If their kids need help, I help them. In this case, I just happen to need back-up."

That quiets the questions for a while. Sierra lapses back into her complaints while Eli and Kalia continue their conversation. Tony does his best to assuage Sierra's discomforts, making it clear that he has quite the crush on her. Unfortunately, Sierra likes her guys upper-scale attractive and, as I said before, Tony is mid-level at best. She repeatedly turns down his efforts despite his best intentions. I can't help but feel bad for the guy.

Eventually, she drops back to walk with Zev. I assume it's because Eli has clearly moved on and she's already mentioned wanting to try with Zev. If only she knew her type was 'werewolf', her shock would be most enjoyable.

I scoot ahead to take her place beside Tony, hoping to soothe his trampled self-esteem some. No one deserves to feel like the type of trash Sierra is so good at making them feel like. He flashes me a smile. "Beautiful day for a hike, isn't it?" He asks.

It really is. The sun is high and bright in a cloudless sky and the temperature's come up quite a bit since this morning. "It's perfect," I agree.

"Did you do much hiking before?"

"Some. My dad used to take us on hikes to build our endurance and stamina as part of our training."

I can see him mentally kicking himself for bringing it up. It's not his fault though. My parents and Dorris were obviously integral parts of both Eli's and my lives. We can't just forget they existed or avoid talking about them. "I'm sorry. I shouldn't have asked," he apologizes.

I smile. "It's fine. It actually helps to talk about them some."

"Really? Are you sure?" He still looks worried.

"Yes. I promise."

His smile returns. "Ok, good."

Behind us, a frustrated growl gets our attention. We turn to see Zev has stopped in his tracks, seething with irritation. Sierra looks at him in shock. "Shut up," he snarls at her.

"I was just saying…"

"I said shut up," he interrupts her.

"Let her explain," Eli butts in.

Zev turns his glare on him. "Stay out of it."

Eli does just the opposite, stalking past us to stand toe to toe with Zev. "Make me."

Zev gathers himself to pounce, but I speak up quickly. "Maybe we should break for lunch," I suggest. Two werewolves with zero meat in their systems is a recipe for disaster. Their anger rose far too quickly to be reasonable.

"I think that's a good idea," Langley agrees, apparently sharing the same thought.

Neither of them budges, glaring daggers at each other like they hope the other might drop dead through eye contact alone. "Eli." I try to get his attention. When that doesn't work, I try one of Dorris's methods, dropping my voice an octave and applying his full name. "Elias Wolfric Thorn."

That succeeds in breaking through to him. He takes half a step back and looks at me. "Lunch time," I say brightly. He glares at Zev once more and then comes to join me for some jerky.

Sierra seems frozen in terror until Zev stalks past her. Across from me, Tony looks between the two werewolves before shaking his head. "That boy's got a death wish," he mutters to himself.

Eli's sulking as he tears into his jerky. I know for most of the group it just looked like a super intense staring contest, but Zev just won. I know enough about canines to know that was a play for dominance and the second Eli stepped down and looked away; he conceded to Zev being dominant. Not alpha, though. That place goes solely to Langley.

I want to cheer him up, but I know it's partly my fault. If I hadn't distracted him, there's a possibility he would have come out on top. But it also could have become physical. I wanted to avoid bloodshed. Like I said, Eli gets mean without protein.

I'm still wracking my brain for something to say when Kalia joins us, flashes her dimpled smile and tells him it was nice of him to stand up for Sierra. Just like that, he's fine again. Feeling totally useless and utterly replaced, I scoot away a bit and nibble my jerky in silence.

Thus, begins my descent into fall back friend, just like with all my so called 'friends' in school. He won't need me or look for me until there's no one else to play with. Then, suddenly, he'll be knocking on my door.

For the rest of the day, Sierra keeps her distance from Zev. That's probably one of her more intelligent moves. After their earlier argument, he seems edgier than usual. Though, that's more likely a result of his face off with Eli than whatever words he exchanged with Sierra.

CHAPTER 10

When we finally stop for the night, I'm too tired to see straight. Again, Zev goes hunting while we set camp and, again, only six bedrolls are laid out. Tony and I have first watch, much to my disappointment. I was so looking forward to closing my eyes for a bit. He keeps trying to talk to me about random things, which I find both helpful and extremely irritating. I'm not in any mood to talk, but his chattering is the only thing keeping me awake.

At switching time, Tony tells me he'll wake Langley. I expected this. For an experienced hunter, he's a serious coward with a huge amount of fear for someone he believes to be human. He can battle werewolves for a living, but God forbid he has to wake Zev.

Part of me wonders if he's as hard to wake as Eli. Maybe it's a werewolf thing. I kneel next to Zev and lightly touch his shoulder, whispering his name. He jerks up-right and I'm met by a knife at my throat, answering my previous question. Zev is an incredibly light sleeper. Realization and then something I might consider to be guilt if it were anyone else, crosses his face.

"Sorry," I whisper. "It's your watch."

He lowers the knife and rises to his feet. "Thanks," He mumbles.

As I'm preparing to wiggle down into the comfort of prewarmed blankets, he turns back. "Amane," He whispers. I look up, thinking I must've done something wrong. Or maybe he just doesn't want me sleeping in his bedroll. "There's a knife in a pocket in there, in case you need it."

"Um, thanks," I answer, feeling slightly confused. First, what a strange place to stash a knife. Second, why is he telling me this? He nods to me and joins Langley on the perimeter.

I finally get to wiggle into the waiting warmth and get comfortable. I don't know if it's possible to fall in love with a smell, but if it is, I just did. Zev's bedroll smells like Earth and leaves in fall and the tang of pine needles. Like it's been bathed in all the scents of the forest. I realize it's strange to pick up such scents from a bedroll while laying in the *actual* forest, but that's exactly how it smells.

I take a deep breath before I realize this is Zev's scent and I'm washed in a wave of embarrassment. No one saw me huffing blankets, and it's not like I'm some obsessed weirdo just waiting for the next whiff of the guy I'm obsessing over. I just *really* love being in the forest and, apparently, Zev happens to smell just like it. But I can't help imagining if someone had noticed. How mortifying that would be?

Despite my exhaustion, sleep is beyond my reach. That terrible feeling of something wrong has settled over me again, keeping me awake and alert. I can tell by the way he's pacing that Zev feels it too. From time to time, Langley joins him, and they murmur to each other, but I can't hear what's being said.

To my surprise, Elias comes to sit by me. He doesn't look at me but scans the darkness. "Do you feel it?" He asks in a whisper.

I sit up so I can join his vigilance. "It feels like it did that night," I answer. He nods.

Langley circles around to crouch in front of us. "You two should be getting some sleep," he says gently.

Eli meets his eyes. "No, we should be up and armed. Something's coming and we're not hiding under blankets this time."

He glances at Zev, who has his back to us on the far side of the fire. "So, you feel it too." Both of us nod. Langley looks at me, puzzled. "And you feel this?"

"Yes, don't you?" How could he not? It's an overwhelming feeling of impending doom.

He shakes his head. "Not like the three of you can, apparently. I know something's off, but it's not enough to wake me or keep me up like it seems to be for you kids."

"We should wake the others and make sure they're ready," Eli tells him.

Langley nods. "Zev was of the same mind. Let's get to it, I guess." At some point, I'm going to have a lot of questions for Langley. He knows more about Eli than he wants to let on. Right now, there are more pressing matters, however. We set to work mobilizing the others, much to their confusion.

Zev and Eli somehow manage to work together to check weapon supplies. For some reason, this makes Langley quite pleased. He keeps casting sparkly-eyed glances their way. "Why does it please you so much when they get along?" I blurt out.

He looks shocked by my outburst and then pretends to put all his attention on packing up. "I don't know what you mean," he claims innocently.

I cross my arms and give him a pointed look. "Sure, you don't."

He sighs and meets my eyes. "If you must know, I firmly believe that if those two can learn to work together, they will be a force to be reckoned with. As it is, Zev is incredibly strong on his own. If he and Elias joined forces, they'd be unstoppable."

The only reason he has for drawing that conclusion is their werewolf blood. Otherwise, why would he be any more interested in them teaming up than anyone else? And, if he knows that Eli is half werewolf, he must know who Eli's father is. Which begs the question; why is he being so evasive about sharing that information with us?

As I said, a lot of questions. I'm still putting my trust in him. He may be keeping more secrets than an international spy, but he was a good friend of my parents. I have to believe he's just doing his best to protect us.

Eli comes to hand me my crossbow. It's loaded and ready for action. "You ready for this?" He asks in a low voice.

"Born ready," I answer.

He smiles. Without even trying, he sees right through my façade. I'm scared shitless at what I feel is coming our way. He gives my shoulder a squeeze. "Remember, we've got a full team this time, and I've always got your back."

I force a smile of my own. "Yeah, I know." But if they get him this time, I'll be completely alone. What am I supposed to do if he's gone?

He moves away to make sure Kalia's ready next. I know he really likes her. I've never seen him act this way around a girl before, which means he sees her as potentially more than a fling. I should be jealous, but I'm not. Not really. I'm actually happy for him. Out of all the girls he's chased over the years, I like Kalia best and I'd be happy to call her part of our minuscule family. As long as I still have my best friend.

I watch them together for another moment as they share a laugh. Then he goes rigid suddenly and his eyes snap to the trees. On my other side, Zev has done the same. It's time to fight.

Without waiting to hear the werewolves myself, I lift my crossbow and fit it against my shoulder. As one, we all back up until we form a circle around our blazing campfire. "Steady," Langley advises. His go-to for calming people's nerves.

I can hear them now, footsteps crunching on the frozen ground and twigs snapping away. I'm trying to be confident and steady, but my breath is coming in ragged gulps and my heart is trying to hammer its way through my ribs. I wonder briefly if my parents felt this way before they were attacked. Did they feel vulnerable, or did they take comfort from each other's presence?

A hand grips my shoulder firmly. "Steady, Amane." I look up to find Zev beside me with his eyes still on the trees. He must smell my fear... or hear my pounding heart. I have to get a grip on myself if I'm to be of any help to anyone. He knows this.

I swallow hard, my throat drier than the desert, and nod. He gives my shoulder a quick squeeze before releasing me and aiming his crossbow as the first of the werewolves burst out of the woods. Another heartbeat later and my fear is forgotten as my training kicks in. There's no time for thinking or fear. To hesitate means to die.

I empty my crossbow and there's no time to reload. I sling it across my back, drawing my twin pistols. I'd stupidly forgotten to reload. Both guns are empty and that mistake nearly costs me my life.

Zev slams into the werewolf that's almost on top of me and knocks it away. "Idiot!" He snarls at me on his way by. Like I needed a reminder of my own stupidity.

I re-holster the guns and grab the closest weapon I can find; a flaming branch from the fire. *Not this again!* I groan inwardly. Next time I'm fighting with proper weapons, dammit!

I swing it with my full weight at the nearest werewolf before he can take a bite out of me. This only seems to piss it off.

I'm angry too. All I wanted was to get some sleep in a delicious smelling bedroll, and these Goddamn man-dogs had to come and ruin that. Now, I'm exhausted, achy, and reduced to battling with a fiery stick. And *he* has the audacity to be mad at *me*?

He lunges and I duck and roll to the side. Coming to my feet beside Sierra, I snatch an expandable spear from her belt, tossing my stick back into the fire. "Hey!" She protests, but I'm not listening.

The werewolf spins to come at me again. Just as he pounces, I hit the button to extend the spear. His momentum drives it through his heart. Before he hits the ground, I've wrenched my weapon free and turned to meet my next opponent.

From there, I lose track of the battle. It's a whirlwind of fur, fire, and flashing weapons. I'm vaguely aware that we are losing ground, and fast. That knowledge pushes me to fight harder, but it doesn't matter. We're outnumbered five to one.

A hand grabs me suddenly and shoves me into the trees. "Run!" Zev snarls at me. For the first time, I hesitate. I can't run and abandon my team. What about Elias? Where is he?

Zev's backing his way towards me, dispatching those who have noticed our retreat. Over his shoulder, I realize the werewolves are herding the others into the trees on the other side of the camp. "GO!" Zev barks.

"But..."

"Amane!" He growls.

Out of sheer luck, I manage to meet Eli's eyes. "Go," he mouths, his eyes a mixture of desperation and determination. That's all the prodding I need. I run.

Moments later, Zev falls in step beside me. He grabs my hand and steers me left. I stumble, find my balance, and continue running. I hear some werewolves following us, spurring me faster.

Abruptly, Zev dives right and slides to the ground, dragging me with him. We fall into a root cave below an ancient oak. He rolls so he's on top of me. "Don't move," he whispers. I'm not really in a position to argue. Truthfully, it's comforting to have his warm weight over me and the solid ground behind me, a cocoon of protection.

Werewolves barrel past us two breaths later. Three sets of feet, the last one stopping in front of us, probably sniffing the air for our scent. I hold my breath and screw my eyes shut, burrowing my face into Zev's shoulder. We're dead, I just know it.

Then the feet move off after the others. I exhale slowly, but we remain motionless for another moment. Finally, Zev shifts off me and peeks outside.

"We should be good for now. Get some rest," he tells me.

"What about the others?" I ask.

"There's nothing we can do right now. We'll track them in the morning."

He's right, I know, but I can't stop worrying. I sit back against the dirt wall and try to calm my thoughts. My adrenaline's still pumping too hard for sleep.

Zev glances back at me and heaves a sigh. "We'll get your boyfriend back tomorrow. Just relax." There's a bitter note in his voice and I wonder if he'd be just as happy to let Eli die. I know they don't get along, but I didn't think they hated each other.

"He's not my boyfriend," I snap back using Eli's standard response. "He's my family." And that's just it. My entire list of family now begins and ends with Elias. I look away as my glare starts to dissolve into tears.

Zev's tone softens about as much as I think it's capable of softening. "Sorry, I just thought…"

"Well, don't," I snap. We fall silent and I'm left to battle my tears before they spill down my face. I lost him. For all my efforts and determination, Eli is gone and now I'm alone.

Eventually, I doze off despite the cold nipping at my extremities now that my adrenaline has worn off. The next thing I know, Zev is nudging me awake. "Amane," he whispers. "Wake up." I open my eyes and he presses a finger to his lips. "I want to show you something,"

I follow him to the entrance of our tiny cave and peer out. Right in front of us is a herd of deer pawing through the snow and pulling bark off the trees. "Wow." I breathe.

"Yeah," he agrees softly. I glance at him, but he's totally absorbed in watching the deer. So, this is a glimpse at the softer side of the most dangerous and terrifying Zev. A smile spreads over my face. I could get used to this side of him.

"We should go," he murmurs, but he doesn't seem inclined to disrupt the deer just yet. After another moment, he releases a long sigh and then hauls himself out into daylight. Instantly, the deer make a break for it, snorting warnings as they leap through the trees. He watches them go while I climb out beside him and then we back-track to camp.

The fire's burned down to smoldering ashes and the place is trashed. The ground is littered with the human bodies of dead werewolves. I swallow a swell of bile rising in my throat and try not to look at the bodies.

"If you have anything valuable, you better grab it," Zev says, back to his usual gruff self.

I locate my pack and check its contents. Everything's still in place, including my parents' journals. My dad's letter is missing, though. Frowning slightly, I search around the ground. It's not super important, I guess. Just sentimental.

Deciding we don't have time to worry about it, I grab Eli's bag to see if he has anything of importance inside. I find his mother's necklace and a picture of her he must have grabbed before we left his house. I stow them securely in my own bag before pulling out my bullets and reloading my pistols.

"That would've been useful last night," Zev says drily. He's checking his and Langley's packs.

"Shut up. I know I screwed up," I tell him.

71

Once we've shouldered our bags, we get down to the business of finding their trail. It's not difficult. With that many of them, they left a clear trail to follow.

I point out some blood on the snow and Zev grunts. "Do you know who that might belong to?" I ask him.

"How would I know that?" He demands, giving me a suspicious look. For all he knows, I could be wondering if he saw who got injured, but I almost let it slip that I know his secret.

I point out a larger patch. "Whoever it is, they're bleeding quite heavily."

All pretense is dropped as he growls. "Langley." His pace picks up and I have to trot to keep up. I may not know much of anything about Zev, but I do know he is fiercely loyal to Langley.

We eat as we go, keeping a steady pace. Even so, I can't shake the feeling that we're losing ground. The blood trail ends about a mile from camp. This seems to cause Zev more concern than seeing the blood. He's quiet and broody as we trudge our way through the trees. More broody than usual.

CHAPTER 11

The day passes without a sign or sound of our comrades. I watch as Zev sinks down against a tree with a growl of frustration, apparently deciding to stop for the night. There's only a little jerky left, which I willingly pass to him.

"You'll have to hunt for your breakfast," I tell him, gnawing on some bread and nuts.

"Aren't there other rations?"

"Yeah, but that's the last of the meat and, no offense, but I'd rather not wander around the forest with you if you have no other meat in your system."

He gives me a quizzical look, but doesn't demand an explanation. He insists on taking first watch. I'm still too reluctant to argue with him or cause him to lose his temper, so I simply curl up on my side and try to get some sleep. We left our bedrolls behind, believing they'd only slow us down and our jackets would be warm enough. Now, I'm regretting that decision, wishing for a cozy place to warm my numb fingers and frosty toes.

I must doze off at some point because when I open my eyes next the sun is beginning to filter through the trees. The second thing I notice is how strong that deep, forest scent is. I push myself up and a jacket slides off to the ground. Zev is still sitting against the tree, now jacketless. He's watching me wake up with an expressionless face.

"You didn't wake me," I say in an accusing tone. He shrugs. That's his entire answer. "Aren't you cold?" Another shrug. I sigh in frustration. "If we come across any of those werewolves and you're tired and sick, it's going to be bad for both of us. In case you haven't noticed, I'm not the strongest fighter."

His expression finally changes, turning to one of mock shock. "Really?"

I roll my eyes at that. "Yes, really."

He rises, donning his jacket and bag. "You shouldn't be so quick to sell yourself short."

I give him a confused look, but he just turns and walks off through the trees. I scramble to catch up and fall into step behind him. Several minutes later, I finally remember my manners.

"Thank you, by the way." He doesn't respond, but I know he heard me.

Roughly four hours later of trudging in silence and trying to fill my mind with any thoughts that don't include dead parents and a now missing Eli, the trail goes cold. We stop and glance around, looking for some sign they passed this way. "Where to now, Wolfie?" I bite my tongue as soon as the words leave my mouth. I have *got* to stop blurting things out!

I can't tell if he's mad or confused as he stares a hole through me. "Don't call me that," he says, finally.

"Sorry," I mumble at my feet.

He looks at the forest ahead and then back at me. "We should eat." He decides. I nod my answer, taking a seat as he drops his pack. "I'll be back in ten." He informs me before stalking off into the woods.

I silently beat myself up while I wait for his return. I really am an idiot. Smart people think before they speak. I wonder if he's really coming back, or if he's finally decided to ditch me.

Just as I'm working myself into a panic, he returns, sitting next to his pack and leveling his eyes at me. "Who told you?"

"Who told me what?" I ask innocently.

"Don't play dumb," he snarls. "Was it Elias?" He's looking at me like he can drill the answer from my brain.

I meet his eyes so he can see I'm being honest. "No, he didn't have to. I already knew."

"How?"

I shrug. "I honestly don't know. I've spent my entire life with a half-blood werewolf as my best friend, and I didn't have an inkling until he showed me. Well, I mean, I guess he always felt a little different from others, but I assumed that's because he was familiar. Now, suddenly, I can pick a werewolf out of a pack of hunters, no problem. I thought that was normal among hunters, but then, Sierra wouldn't have been pursuing either of you so intently and more experienced hunters probably would have killed you ages ago. So, I don't know."

He's quiet for a long moment as he studies my face before he nods. I guess he accepts my answer. "Don't call me Wolfie, or Wolf Boy. I don't like it."

"Noted," I answer. Then, because I still haven't learned to keep my mouth shut, I say, "What about 'Sir Wolfington'?" My inquiry is met with a cold glare. "So that's a no."

I guess I have a death wish because then I'm asking another question I should not be asking. "Zev literally means wolf. Doesn't that bother you?"

He looks away. "I didn't pick it." He stands and shoulders his pack, signaling the end of our conversation. He didn't really answer my question though. "Let's go," he grunts.

"You should eat."

"I already did."

I cringe at the prospect of what that means. We don't have a fire and he wasn't gone long enough to cook anything. "Gross," I say mostly to myself.

A flicker of humor crosses his eyes. "You can handle a camp full of dead werewolves, but one raw squirrel makes you squeamish?"

"No one was eating the werewolves," I argue, falling into step behind him. "Never mind, I don't want to think about it." Sometimes I have a very vivid imagination and at this time it's decided to create images of dead werewolves being gnawed on by wild animals. "You should probably get checked for worms, though." I can't see his face, but I could swear he chuckles at that.

My brain slides back to our earlier conversation. "Did you tell Langley about Elias?"

"No," he answers defensively, like I'm accusing him of something. "Well, I'm pretty sure he knows."

"Did he say something?" Is that a hint of jealousy I hear? Like Langley would tell me anything he wouldn't tell Zev.

"No, but he's awfully keen on partnering you two up even though you can't stand each other. He thinks you and Eli would be unstoppable together, but as far as I know, he doesn't know Eli from Adam so, I think he knows about Eli's werewolf blood. Plus, if he doesn't know, why on Earth is he hauling us up a werewolf infested mountain? I think he knows a hell of a lot more than he's telling anyone."

"Maybe." The answer is quiet, like he's brooding again. His steps start to slow and then he stops. When I draw up beside him, I find his expression to be a thoughtful one, if not a little hurt.

"You alright there, Atlas?" My heart does a funny skip when I use Eli's nickname on Zev, as though I've betrayed him in some way. But that look is so much like Eli's that it's hard to resist.

He blinks out of his reverie and looks at me. "What?"

"Atlas, you know, the dude who carries the world on his shoulders?"

He shakes his head. "I'm fine," he says gruffly, before crunching away again. He stops so suddenly that I crash into him. "You think we're an infestation? Like some parasite that needs to be removed?" I can't tell if he's confused, hurt, or angry. It's such an odd tone, especially for him. And after he basically growled about being fine.

"That's not what I meant. I just mean, as in there's a lot of werewolves on these mountains. Like, there are a lot of hunters in these mountains. An infestation of hunters."

He turns away without a word and trudges away. I can't shake this feeling I hurt his feelings by calling werewolves an infestation. It seems like such a little thing, a simple misplaced word. Is he actually a sensitive guy?

The trees open to reveal a frozen lake just before dusk. Zev pauses at the water's edge and looks out across it. "Do you think they really crossed this?" I ask. It seems pretty sketchy at this time of year in my opinion. I know the weather's different here in the mountains, but Spring is still well on its way.

"I know they did," he says. He drops his bag off his shoulders and rummages through it until he finds a coiled length of rope. Uncoiling it, he steps forward to wrap one end around my waist. My heart flutters in my chest at the feel of his arms around me and I have to stop myself from breathing him in like the weird, obsessive girl I was so embarrassed to look like the other night.

"What are you doing?" I ask, hoping he doesn't hear the catch in my throat.

"Tying you to me."

Oh, ok. "Why?"

He meets my eyes as he cinches the knot tight around my middle. "If one of us goes through, the rope will catch us."

"A herd of people *just* crossed, and it doesn't look like they had an issue." I point out.

He's tying his own end now. "Yes, a herd of people just crossed the ice in early Spring. We have no way of knowing what kind of condition they left it in."

"Oh."

He shoulders his pack once more and we begin our cautious crossing. Slowly, I begin to gain confidence in the ice's sturdiness, and I pick up my pace. Until I take a step and a cracking sound follows. Spiderweb-like cracks spread out in all directions from my foot. "Zev."

Zev turns back with a glare when he gets jerked back by the taut line. Realizing my predicament, the glare melts away and I can almost see his mind whir into action. "Steady," he cautions as an automatic response. Gee, I wonder who he was raised by. "Very slowly, try to get down on your hands and knees."

I start to get down and the cracks spread further. I freeze in an awkward crouch. "Amane, you need to distribute your weight." Zev urges, his voice carrying a hint of urgency. Again, I shift lower. And then the ice shatters out from under me and I plunge into the freezing water beneath. Just before my head goes under, I hear Zev yell my name.

I gasp in a lung full of water at the shock of the cold and then my line goes tight again. My body takes over since my brain is in shock, and I propel myself up through the hole. In a surge of water, I resurface and grab frantically for the edge of the ice.

Zev is holding the line tight so I don't slip back under, but he doesn't dare move closer to offer a hand. If we both go under, we're screwed. "Amane, look at me." It's an order. I meet his eyes. "Calm your breathing," he advises.

"Screw you," I answer through gasping breaths and chattering teeth. That's not very nice of me, but he's not the one taking a swim in a frozen lake.

"I'm serious. Breathe." He's being very chill about my spiteful words, remaining calm. I do my best to follow his advice. "Now, kick your feet up behind you. You need to swim out, ok?" It's a slow process, bringing my feet up and then squirming and kicking my way back up onto the ice.

Finally, I'm out. I lay panting on my stomach, willing warmth back into my body. It's no use. The shivering won't stop, and I can't feel anything.

"Get up. We need to get off the ice," Zev presses. I just want to sleep. "Amane, please." His tone is pleading, worried. That alone spurs me into action, army crawling my way to him. Zev isn't the type to worry, so it must be important.

We make it to the other side without further incident. As soon as we're tucked back into the trees, Zev becomes a flurry of activity. My brain is too sluggish to comprehend what's happening and I just sink down until I'm sitting.

He shoves some clothes into my arms. "Change into these while I get a fire going." I doze off and then he's shaking me awake. "Damnit, Amane, you can't sleep. Not yet." He doesn't look angry, despite his tone. He looks... scared?

He studies me for a minute, looking as though he is weighing something in his mind. I feel myself becoming listless. This seems to trigger his decision. "I'm sorry," he whispers, "you'll forgive me later." I'm confused until he starts cutting off my clothes. I'd argue, but I'm shivering too hard. Within minutes he has me fully garbed in an extra set of his own, dry clothes.

He carries me to the fire, laying me on a bed of leaves he must have gathered before stripping off his jacket and draping it over me, making sure to put both hoods over my head. He feeds the fire some more wood and then wedges down between me and the tree, pulling me against his chest.

I can feel his warmth against my back, seeping through my layers. Craving more of it, I wiggle back into him, his arms tightening around me and providing still more warmth. Finally, I'm allowed to sleep. It's dark and dreamless and full of warmth.

CHAPTER 12

I blink awake to the grey light of dawn. Zev is still wrapped around me, his heat filling my body. His breathing is deep and even against my back, telling me he's asleep. It's the first time he's slept in the last forty-eight hours, so I do my best to stay still and not wake him.

For a long time, I doze on and off, enjoying the warmth and the smell surrounding me. It feels like almost an hour before Zev begins to stir. He shifts a little and then I feel him freeze. I think he forgot I was here. "Shit," he swears softly.

"Sorry," I mumble, moving to stand.

"No, not you." I stop, still sitting on the ground beside him. "I shouldn't have fallen asleep." He explains, pushing up to a better sitting position.

I look at him like he's daft because he must be. "You've been up for two days straight. You were bound to fall asleep at some point."

Seeming to realize just how close we are, he stands and begins gathering things. "It's basic training; Always be alert."

I get up and help him gather everything. It seems he emptied my pack at some point and laid everything out to dry. "Well, now you can be extra alert for whatever today brings." I come to my parents' journals and suck in a sharp breath.

Zev is immediately braced for attack, knife in hand. "What? What's wrong?"

I shake my head, trying to swallow back my tears. "Sorry, it's nothing." They're ruined. Most of the pages disintegrated from the water. The writing was washed out of those pages still intact.

He relaxes. "They were important." It's more of a statement than a question.

I nod. "They belonged to my parents." I let out a long, shaky sigh, reminding myself they're objects before setting them aside.

"I'm sorry." His gentle tone has me wondering where Zev has gone and who this imposter is.

I clear my throat and continue picking up my gear. "We should get moving." Moments later, we're on the trail again. My boots are soggy, and I'm still dressed in Zev's clothes, but at least I'm at a normal temperature again.

"Thank you for last night," I say. He doesn't answer. Maybe no one ever taught him how to accept thanks. "How did you know how to get out? And how to get my temperature back to normal?"

"Langley." Back to one-word answers and overwhelming silences.

"Was it part of your training?"

"No."

Grr! He makes it so hard to get to know him. He seemed so open for a brief window and now he's closed himself off again. He could expand just a bit. "So, what exactly is Langley to you?"

He stops to give me a look that suggests I should know the answer to that question. "He is my pack." Not part of his pack, his whole pack. It looks like we're both trying to rescue what's left of our tiny families.

The sun tells me it's nearly ten when Zev stops abruptly. He tilts his head, listening. "We're close," he tells me quietly. Finally!

"Can I ask you something?" I ask as we continue.

"Quietly," he whispers.

I drop my voice to match his. "Why did you help me get away that night? Why not someone else?"

There's a long pause before he answers. "You were the closest one to me and the easiest to pull away."

Ah, no other option. I'd be lying if I said I wasn't a little disappointed. Not that I'm not grateful. Just once, I'd like it if someone actually picked me for me, though. I wonder sometimes if Eli would have even picked me if we hadn't grown up together in the first place.

"Why'd you lay on top of me?" I wish there was a less awkward way of phrasing that question.

"To cover your scent. Mine's harder to find." That makes sense, I suppose, especially based on his natural body odor. "You smell strong enough to stick out like a sore thumb," he adds.

I huff. It's not my fault I haven't been able to shower in almost a week. "You're no rose," I retort.

"It's not bad," he amends quickly. "Just... not werewolf."

"Oh." Now I'm embarrassed. "I lied anyway," I grumble. "You smell freaking fantastic." He smiles at that. A beautiful expression that sparkles in his eyes and lights his entire face. My heart skips unexpectedly.

Within the hour, we come to a ledge that slopes down to a cave. There are a couple dozen people milling about below as they make camp. My gut tells me they're werewolves. We do a quick survey and then fall back to strategize. Thankfully, the wind is blowing our scent away from the camp.

Zev is dead set against me entering the camp under any circumstance, and I'm against him going in alone. In the end, it's decided that I will provide a distraction so he can slip in and free our teammates. A more experienced pair may have come up with a better plan, but it's the best Zev and I can come up with.

I have to skirt the camp until I'm in a position where they can smell me, hoping to draw the majority away. Then I just need to avoid capture and get back up the slope. Should be easy... right?

I slip down the slope until I feel I'm in a good position, then I yell for extra measure. A heartbeat later, I hear underbrush being smashed aside. With a little thrill of excitement, I take off back the way I came. I hope enough of them are coming after me.

Just when I think I'm going to get away, a clawed hand grabs my wrist. I reel around and slam my elbow into the attacker's face, loosening their grip and drawing a yelp from them. I'm free and running again.

Another werewolf breaks through the undergrowth ahead and snarls. I pull out the spear I stole from Sierra, extending it to its full length. More werewolves surround me.

"Shit!" I curse to myself. They lunge and I whirl into action. It's a futile battle. There are too many of them, but I refuse to go down without a fight.

Predictably, I'm overpowered and thrown to the ground. They tie my hands behind my back and shove me back towards their camp. I curse myself the whole way, knowing I failed everyone. I take some consolation from the knowledge that I injured some of them.

In the camp, Zev is already tied and on his knees. A beautiful young woman stands before him with a less-than-lovely sneer, which he returns with a scowl. With the exception of her waist-length, silver hair, she looks like a female Zev.

She brightens at my approach, her sneer turning into a smile. "Looky, brother, they've found your girl." I'm forced to my knees beside him. I guess that explains the resemblance. "I should thank you for bringing her here," she continues.

"Don't touch her," Zev growls low, the words rumbling up from deep in his throat.

She bends so they're eye to eye. "Is she dear to you, Wolfie?" Without so much as a twitch of warning, her hand flashes out and slams into the side of my face, whipping my head to the side in a stinging flash of pain. Now I know why he hates that nickname.

Zev snarls and lunges, but the others beat him down. "Tut tut, Wolfie, that's no way to say hi to your twin. And after we've been apart for so long," she scolds with a mock pout. Zev's answer is another growl.

"Where are our friends?" I ask, interrupting their reunion.

She smiles wolfishly. "Waiting in the cave. Care to join them?"

"Let her go, Arya," Zev warns. Her smile becomes indulgent just before her foot meets my gut. I fold over, gasping for breath as Zev attempts another lunge.

"Zev, stop," I gasp out. He's putting up quite a fight, but I don't understand why. He generally seems to barely tolerate me, so why make such a fuss over a few smacks?

When he ignores me and continues to fight, I draw myself up and square my shoulders, aiming a hard glare at him. The pain in my abdomen makes this harder than usual. "Zev Devante Lycidas!" I use the tone I adopted from Dorris, hoping it works as well on Zev as it did on Elias. "That's enough." He stops instantly and sinks back down beside me.

"That's right. Be a good pup. You've become so well trained." Arya taunts him. His jaw clenches and his glare could stop a heart cold.

"What do you want with us?" I ask her. Besides our imminent deaths.

"Oh, you're disposable." She flashes me a pleasant smile. "I just wanted to meet Wolfie's mate before he watches you die."

I can't stop the laugh that bubbles out of me at that. "I'm not his mate. What on Earth gave you that idea? Do you really think a guy like Zev would look twice at a girl like me? He's so far out of my league it's ridiculous."

For once, her smile falters. "But... his smell is all over you."

"No shit! I fell in the lake and had to borrow his clothes." And, also steal his body heat for the night, but that information would not help our current situation.

She shakes her head as though she can shake away her mistake. "No matter. I'm only here for my brothers. The rest of you can die, for all I care."

Zev's head comes up sharply. "Brothers?" He repeats, accentuating the plural.

"Of course, you and that disgusting half-breed we're forced to share blood with."

She can't mean... "Elias." The word chokes out of me.

A slow smile creeps over her face again. "So, you do belong to one of them." She turns to one of her companions. "Would you fetch my baby brother? Perhaps he will enjoy the show." The man disappears into the cave.

"Why are you doing this?" Zev asks, sounding both defeated and angry.

"Because I'd know the smell of an Ichinose anywhere and, believe me, they have it coming to them. I'm just lucky enough to have caught the one whose demise will hurt both my brothers.

"As to why I've captured you, Father wants to kill you and the mutt. You two are the natural heirs to the pack, and he's not fond of competition. He's been kicking out any males that come of age to challenge him.

"I'd kill you for him, but he insists on doing it himself. It's a matter of pride, I guess, so I have to make do with causing what pain I can before we get there. Starting with this pathetic excuse for a hunter."

Elias stumbles out of the cave and falls on his side at that moment. Arya grins broadly. "This is going to be fun."

As soon as he is up on his knees, she calls to him. "Look baby brother, we found your mate."

Eli's eyes lock onto me, and cold terror flashes through them before he hardens himself. "She's not my mate. She's my sister. My *only* sister."

I watch as she stiffens at the verbal smack. He's rejecting her kinship in favor of a filthy hunter. She lets out a frustrated growl and looks between the three of us. "One of you is lying!"

Suddenly, she's so close to me our noses are almost touching. Beside me, Zev moves to shoulder her away, but another werewolf holds him in place. "It's you, I believe," she tells me. She draws back slightly to eye Zev. "Yes."

Then she straightens. "It doesn't really matter, though, does it? Sister, friend, mate, they'll still mourn you when you're gone. And me, well, I'll enjoy every moment of their torment after the lifetime of it I've had because of them." She surveys the surrounding faces. "Who's hungry?"

Wolfish grins spread across every face in the camp. Two men step forward and yank me to my feet. "I said, don't touch her!" Zev roars in the same instant Eli shouts, "No!" and throws himself at the werewolf beside him.

Zev's on his feet faster than I can blink. He gives himself over to his werewolf form, and he's positively massive. With a wrenching yank, his rope falls away, and he grabs the nearest man by the throat, sinks his claws in, and rips it out. His fangs sink into the next man's throat, causing him to release me. Before the man's body hits the ground, Zev has slashed through my rope.

Every werewolf in camp is now in wolf form, except Eli. I run for him, fumbling with his ties before finally getting them loose. Glancing at the melee, I see Zev and Arya battling it out.

"Get the others out," Eli orders. I start to protest, knowing what he's planning, but he's already throwing himself into the fight, lending Zev backup. Realizing the last place I want to be is in the middle of a fight between werewolf siblings, I take his advice and hurry inside to free our comrades.

They're all tied up in a back corner of the cave. Besides having their hands tied, they're otherwise free. I pause when I catch sight of Langley. He's stretched out along the floor with a large blood stain spread over one side of his body. His face is deathly pale, and his breathing is shallow.

"He's alive," John answers my unspoken question. "Just barely."

I'm spurred back into action at this confirmation. "We have to go. Zev and Eli are buying us time, but I don't know how long they will last."

I untie John first and he helps me release the others. "Thank God, you're ok," Tony says, "when I heard Zev was a werewolf, I could only imagine what he was doing to you out there. I thought for sure he'd have eaten you."

"He's saved my life more than once," I tell him, barely concealing the anger swelling inside me at his unchecked prejudice.

With everyone free of their bonds, John and Tony support Langley between them so we can make our retreat. He rouses enough to help support some of his weight, but not enough to be aware of what's going on. Outside, the fight is still going on in earnest.

I usher my comrades around the side of the cave and direct them towards the ridge. Kalia is the last out of the cave and she freezes at the sight of the werewolves. "Kalia, we have to move," I remind her.

"What about Elias?" She whispers forlornly.

I glance at the werewolves. "He's right behind us." My gut is telling me that's a lie, but I need Kalia to keep going. Eli would have my head if anything happens to her. I can't think about the fact that I'm leaving my family behind for the second time this week. I'd fall apart and he and Zev both need me to stay strong right now.

"Yeah." She nods. "He'll be ok." She's reassuring herself more than anything. I hope with every part of my being that she's right. She turns away to follow the others.

I start to follow her when a strong, furred arm wraps around my waist, turning me so I'm between its owner and the cave wall. I feel the werewolf shudder as it is hit by what I assume was a projectile of some sort. Then the smell of him floods my senses. "Zev," I squeak out.

The arm is becoming human now. "I'm fine, go," he growls in my ear, his forehead pressed to the stone as he tries to push through the pain. "Go!" He repeats when I hesitate.

I place my forehead against the side of his head. "I'm coming back for you," I whisper before pulling away and going after the others, only realizing as I pull away that the projectiles were 2 knives that are now sunk into his back.

We make it over the ridge and down the other side, putting as much space between us and the werewolves as possible while hauling an injured person. I find mine and Zev's packs right where we left them and pass the lighter one to Kalia as we flee. It's mid-afternoon when we finally stop. I don't expect we'll be followed. In the end they got who they wanted.

Zev's pack has a first aid kit we can use for Langley. It also holds my parents' journals set neatly on top of the gear. Why would he have grabbed these?

John works on patching Langley up while the girls and I gather firewood, and Tony does some hunting. He returns with plants and berries, his version of hunting, I guess. It's not much of a meal, but at least it's something.

"So, are you making some kind of fashion statement?" Sierra asks, eyeing my oversized outfit.

I look down at myself and pluck at my shirt. "No, they're Zev's. I fell in the lake and it was all we had." I feel my cheeks color at the memory of how I wound up in these.

She wrinkles her nose in disgust. "You're wearing werewolf clothes? Aren't you afraid you'll get fleas or something?"

My flush fades as I meet her gaze. "How's your face feeling, Sierra?" I deadpan. She fidgets, clearing her throat and focusing on her meager rations.

Kalia lets out a small groan. "Where *are* they? They should be here by now." Nobody answers. No one wants to break the news to her, so we all just exchange quiet glances. Her eyes settle on me. "You said he was right behind us," she says accusingly.

"Kalia, we needed to get out of there," I explain.

Her face screws up into an angry glare while also trying not to cry. "But we should've helped them. How could you just leave him there? Don't you care at all?"

I blink back tears of my own. Of course, I care. It's killing me that I'm here and safe and he's there, a captive and most likely injured. "How can you even call yourself his friend?" She continues. "He counts on you to have his back and you just run. Twice now, you've run rather than stood by him."

"Shut up," I whisper, choking back my tears.

"No! This is your fault!" She pushes.

"Shut up!" I scream at her. "You think you own the monopoly on caring for Eli? Because what? Because you've gotten close this week? That's my *brother*, God dammit! He is *everything* I have left in this world! Yes, I ran away. He *told* me to run, but I'd have to be dead and buried before anyone could stop me from going back for him."

Kalia blinks in surprise at my outburst, her eyes wide with shock. "I'm sorry, I didn't..."

"Screw you," I interrupt her before storming away.

Eventually, she comes looking for me, sitting quietly beside me for a long time. "I am *so* sorry," she says, breaking the silence. "I was so far out of line. There are no excuses for my behavior. I hope you can forgive me."

I wipe a sleeve across my face to dry the tears, and sniffle. "I'm sorry I couldn't help him," I answer thickly.

She looks stricken that I would be apologizing. "Oh, Amane, no, don't apologize. We all know you would have fought for him if you could have."

I nod and sniff again. "I'm going to get him back. Him and Zev."

She smiles gently and gives my hand a squeeze. "*We* will. You're not as alone as you think you are, Amane." I return the hand squeeze. I needed to hear that.

John takes the first watch since he wants to make sure Langley is stable before he turns in. Sierra grumbles about the lack of bedding and tosses and turns for what feels like forever. Tony tries to snuggle up against my back. I have no idea what gave him the notion that this was okay. I get up and find a place beside Kalia, finally getting to sleep with our backs pressed together for warmth.

CHAPTER 13

Langley is awake when the sun comes up. I'm so relieved I almost start crying again. I can only imagine how Zev would feel if he lost Langley.

At first, he just looks around in a state of confusion. Then he sits up suddenly, his eyes going wide. "Where are the boys?" He demands in a panic.

John eases him back down. "They've been taken. We're going to get them back, but first, you need to rest."

Langley tries to push John's hands away. "There's no time for that. We need to get them back."

"There's a little time," I pipe up. "Arya's taking them to their father, so they'll be alive until then, at least. But then, you already knew that." I don't even try to keep the accusation out of my voice. Maybe it's not entirely fair, but I feel like a lot of this could have been avoided if he'd just been honest with us from the very beginning.

He meets my cold glare. "Amane, I..."

I shake my head. "Don't. Just rest now. Later, you're going to tell me everything you know, no more excuses and no more lies." Part of me wonders when I got brave enough to order Langley around, but most of me is just sick to death of being kept in the dark by him.

He swallows, nods and lays back. I try not to look shocked that he actually listened to me. "Ok. It's time you knew." As though that's not obvious.

"Pretty sure the right time would have been before you led us all into the mountains," I remark. He just closes his eyes and turns his head away. Within minutes he's sound asleep.

We spend the morning puttering around camp and conserving our energy. John tries his hand at hunting this time, returning with a rabbit and a couple of grouse. I quietly celebrate that we aren't going to have to make a meal out of Tony's weeds again.

We're running low on ammo now, down to just what I have in my gun and the box in my bag. Both mine and Zev's crossbows, along with Eli's sword, were left behind in the camp where the werewolves invaded. Sierra had a clear enough head to grab some of the blades that were close at hand in the cave, but aside from those, my twin pistols, and the extendable spear, we're mostly unarmed.

Anxiety begins to set in as the sun climbs steadily higher into the sky and I find myself pacing without having consciously decided to. I can't explain how, but I can feel the werewolves moving away. It's like there's an invisible string connecting me to Elias and Zev, twin flames burning on the edge of my awareness. I had hoped the pack would stay put, but it obviously makes sense that they would be moving away.

Kalia falls into step beside me. "A penny for your thoughts?" She asks brightly.

I open my mouth and then close it, unsure how to articulate what I'm feeling. "Do you feel that?" I ask instead.

She pauses as though searching her senses. "Feel what?"

"They're getting away. I can feel them slipping through our fingers.

She frowns. "It's just anxiety. Try to relax."

I shake my head. "It's more than anxiety. The longer we wait here, the further away they get."

"Maybe…" she begins, pausing to sigh and look at her hands. "Maybe it's your connection to Elias. I've heard of such things in werewolf packs. The alpha can sense where its mate is." She flips her hair over her shoulder and glances at the trees, struggling to put her thoughts into words. "You two are so close. Maybe that's what you're feeling."

"We aren't mates," I point out. "We're family."

She attempts a smile that doesn't reach her eyes. "Yeah, well, still. It's the only thing that makes sense with what you're describing."

It would make sense if it was just Eli I was sensing. But it's also Zev, and I have no explanation for that. None that I'm ready to admit to yet, anyhow. Stupid emotions! I wish they'd stop being all over the place and just settle back to that even keel I'd always known before.

Langley begins to stir, drawing our attention away from our quiet meeting. He groans and pushes himself into a sitting position. The camp's occupants all crowd around him, eager to provide him with anything he may need, not that we have much to offer.

His eyes land on Sierra. "I need water." She scurries away to find one of the almost empty canteens.

She hurries back, and he takes a long swallow. I hang back, doing my best not to bombard him with questions. He is recovering from the brink of death, after all. He sighs, looks at Tony, and says he needs food. Tony obliges.

After a few mouthfuls of rabbit, he finally meets my gaze. "Ok, let's talk." I sigh, releasing a breath I hadn't realized I was holding, and take a seat on the ground in front of him.

"I want to know everything," I tell him. "Even your relationship with Dorris, and what you know of Zev's past. All of it."

He closes his eyes to organize his thoughts. When he opens them again, he plunges into his tale. "Dorris and I were lovers. More than lovers. We had plans to start a family together, that is, until she was raped by a werewolf.

"I thought she should abort. Nothing good could come from that man's loins. Of course, she refused. Elias was, despite how he was conceived, a miracle baby. The doctors had all said she would never bear children, and she loved that boy fiercely from the moment she realized she carried him.

"We planned to raise him together. She couldn't stay here, though. She had to leave, and she had to hide any trace of his existence. Otherwise, his father would have hunted him down and killed him before he was old enough to walk. If the hunters didn't get to him first.

"Your parents always planned to go with us. We had been a team for nearly ten years at that point, our entire hunting career, and we'd known each other even longer. It made sense to them that we would continue to be a team, even outside of the business.

"Then we heard rumors of another child. One that had been born to the werewolf's mate, who apparently passed away during the delivery. We didn't know where the child was, but we knew he wasn't safe and Dorris was adamant that he belonged with his brother. So, I stayed behind to find the missing child while Dorris and your parents went on ahead.

"Benjamin caught word of Dorris's child and his... less than savory roots. Somehow, he'd learned we were leaving. He black mailed me into staying. He said as long as I stayed, Elias's existence would remain a secret within the business, but if I left, he'd send hunters to eliminate the potential threat. It was the only way he could get me to stay, and it worked like a charm. I cut all ties to Dorris to keep them safe.

"I continued my search for Zev, quietly, staying under the radar. It took me years, too many years. When I finally found him, he was almost ten. He'd spent the majority of his life in a cage, fed on scraps and beaten for existing. Those who held him captive planned to someday set him loose on his father. A rival pack hoping to join the two by eliminating the other's alpha.

"It was another year before he trusted me enough to speak to me. He was jumpy then, always expecting a beating. When I offered to teach him how to fight, he jumped at the opportunity, though he already knew some. Zev has always been stronger than any child I've known, mentally speaking. He didn't want to be scared anymore, and he thought knowing how to fight would help him feel more secure.

"He learned faster than I anticipated. At sixteen, Benjamin decided he was ready for the field. I argued, but Zev insisted he was ready. The other kids were frightened of him, so he didn't have any friends. I think he believed he could impress them... or escape them. He's not a warm person, always putting up walls to keep people out.

"Benjamin doesn't know about Zev. As far as he knows, Zev is the orphan of hunters, and I took him off the streets. I raised Zev as my own, just like Dorris had wanted. It was... trying. He's a werewolf after all, and they are stubborn, hotheaded creatures. But I love him just the same.

"And then you two showed up practically on our doorstep. It was bittersweet. I should have been there to fight beside Dorris and your parents, but you two were safe and whole. It was my job to keep you that way. And to see Elias and Zev together at last… it was a dream come true in its own twisted way.

"I thought perhaps with both the boys together, they could take out their father and end his tyranny once and for all. Men like him are why werewolves are given such bad names.

"I couldn't tell Elias who his father was because I didn't want him tearing off after the man in hopes of some fairy-tale ending. And I thought if he knew everything, he'd be less willing to face him, or too willing to face him. I needed him to have a cool head for this mission."

"Why didn't you tell him you were his father? He was all ready to believe you were," I ask.

"I guess… I was worried maybe Dorris had changed her mind about that. Maybe she'd move on or decided to hate me for bailing. It was because of my own fear."

I let this information settle into my brain, filing it away. So, Benjamin *had* known that Dorris had a child, and it was all an act when he met Eli. What kind of man keeps a family apart for his own gain like that?

"Did Zev know what your intentions were?"

"Zev knew we were looking for Eli's father. I never told him that he and Elias were brothers. He would have made too many other connections from that information, and I'm fairly certain Benjamin bugged my office."

I nod my understanding and squint up at the sky. This is a lot to take in. "And Zev's sister, did you know about her?"

"Yes, I actually spent some time searching for her as soon as Zev trusted me enough to mention her name. It turns out, he was born first and whisked away to what they thought was a safe place, before the midwife realized there was a second child coming. I certainly never thought she'd be an issue with this mission.

"I think Zev knew, however. I believe he's been in contact with her several times over the years, but for some reason he never felt comfortable sharing this with me. He's been edgier on this mission, though, so I believe he expected to see his sister."

Langley looks tired again. I need time to process all of this and he needs more rest. "Thank you," I say. "You should get some more sleep."

"But what about getting Elias and Zev back?" Kalia asks. "We're losing ground, aren't we?"

Langley gives her a puzzled look. "Losing ground? What are you talking about?"

"They're on the move," I explain. "I think we still have a little time, though."

He looks between us. "How do you know this?"

Kalia and I share a look. "She can sense Elias pulling away." She confesses. I don't mention also sensing Zev's departure.

"That's not possible," he argues. "Unless... It's been known to happen between werewolf mates. Not among hunters."

Kalia shakes her head. "We don't understand it either. Hunters don't usually sense werewolves."

"I do." I hadn't meant to say that out loud, but since we're sharing secrets, I guess it's fitting. Everyone turns to look at me, and I shrug. "What? I thought it was normal."

"It's not," Tony answers flatly.

"When did you discover this?" Langley asks.

"When I first saw Zev in the cafeteria." I look at Sierra. "Remember, I asked how many werewolves were employed by the hunters?"

"Yeah, but I didn't think... He was on the other side of the room!"

I shake my head. "It isn't important now. We should let Langley rest." Langley agrees with a grunt. Everyone grudgingly vacates his area. He stops me before I get too far.

"Why didn't you say anything if you knew what Zev was?"

I shrug again. "I thought if I mentioned Zev, he'd mention Elias. As long as I held my tongue, they were both safe."

"Thank you."

I smile without feeling. "It was purely personal."

Langley slips off to sleep once more and we resume our restless pacing. Slowly I come to realize that we're all waiting on Langley to form a plan. He's not in any condition to do this, however. It's up to us. Langley is too injured for more than returning to base.

For too long, I've relied on others to do the thinking; my parents, Eli, Zev, Langley. I can't afford to do that any longer. I can't hide behind Eli anymore. All this time I've leaned far too heavily on him.

When Langley wakes next, I have a plan. I barely give him time to stir before launching it at him. Not one of my most patient moves. Predictably, he does not approve. It involves him and John returning to headquarters while we four younger hunters go after Zev and Elias.

"No," he says flatly. "You're just kids. I won't allow it."

I sit back and cross my arms over my chest. "You should've thought of that before bringing 'just kids' as your team for this mission."

He gives me a measuring look. "You can't go alone. Tony's the only one with enough field training." I start to protest, but he holds up his hand to stop me. "John and I will go with you. I just need a little more time."

"We don't have time!" I snap and immediately bite my tongue. I shouldn't be yelling at our leader.

For a minute he just looks at me, and then his expression softens. "We're going to get your family back, Amane. Just give me tonight and we will go tomorrow."

I don't want to agree with his terms. What if tomorrow is too late? They're being led to their deaths and we're just waiting. Langley's right, though. The girls and I don't have the field training to take on a pack of werewolves.

I release a long breath. "Fine, but if you die from your own stubbornness, Zev will never forgive you."

He smiles. "Let me worry about Zev. You just concentrate on getting Elias back."

As though the two are mutually exclusive. Why does no one seem to understand that I want Zev back just as much as I want Eli back? It's not like I've excluded Zev from any of my thoughts on their rescue. Inside, I feel them both as a strong pull on my gut, equally intense and equally important. I have to find them. Both of them.

Sleep is an elusive mistress. Every time I close my eyes images of what Zev and Eli might be going through tramp through my mind. Giving up, I join Tony on the watch.

He smiles at me. "Couldn't sleep?"

I shake my head. "No, too anxious."

"I'm sure he'll be ok, he does have werewolf blood, after all. They tend to be less murderous of their own kind."

I don't know how to respond to that. The pack that took them intends to kill them in order to ensure their alpha's continued reign. But maybe they'll change their minds and decide to integrate them into the pack. I know that's wishful thinking, but I have to keep hoping for the best.

We sit in silence until Tony clears his throat awkwardly. "I... uh... I want to tell you something. We don't know how tomorrow is going to go and I want you to know, in case... Well... In case we don't make it back."

I believe I know where this is going, but I say, 'ok', to encourage him. I'd like to know for sure before making a fool out of myself.

"I like you," he says, doing his best to not look at me. "Like, I *really* like you and, if we make it out of this alive, I would very much like to date you."

I should be flattered. Never in my life has a guy professed to have feelings for me. But I'm not his first choice. He likes me because I've been nice to him, that's all. He should be confessing his feelings to Sierra. Besides, Tony has the potential to be a good friend, but nothing more.

"Girls aren't usually nice to you, are they?" I ask.

He looks taken aback. "What? Where did that come from?"

I smile at him. "Tony, I'm flattered, but I'm not dumb. I've seen how girls treat you, particularly Sierra. If Sierra treated you as a human being just once, we would not be having this conversation. I know you like her, I mean, look at her. She's gorgeous. So, thank you, but I'm going to have to decline. You should try pursuing someone you're truly interested in."

Another long silence follows, and then he sighs. "Ok, I'm sorry." I don't know what he's apologizing for. It was nice of him to consider me.

My thoughts wander, swirling into confusing patterns. The werewolves have stopped moving away. I hope that, wherever they are, they've reached their destination. Neither Langley nor Zev are in any condition to be traipsing through the mountains any more than we already have. I can still see the look on Zev's face when those blades found their mark. Is he even alive still?

I push the thought away. Of course he is. I wouldn't sense a dead werewolf... Right? We need to stay positive. And, according to Sierra's mumbled dreams, she's positive we're all going to die. That's reassuring.

If the werewolves have reached their destination, have Eli and Zev faced their father? If they were dead, would I know? Are they strong enough to defeat him if he chooses to fight fair?

With Zev's injuries, I'm inclined to think not. Elias is strong, but he's only half werewolf and he hasn't had to fight too many purebloods, and never an alpha. I think it's safe to assume alphas are incredibly strong if they keep an entire werewolf pack in line.

CHAPTER 14

I finally fell asleep at some point during John's shift. Kalia wakes me to the gray light of dawn. "We're preparing to move out. Langley says you're on point. He thinks your connection to Elias could help lead us to them."

I sit up, stretch, and rub the sleep from my eyes. John's jacket slips off my shoulder to land on the ground. "I hope he's right." I tell her, staring at the jacket. Zev and Eli may very well be naked out there. Werewolves shed their clothes when they shift forms, but then, maybe the cold doesn't affect them the way it affects humans. Zev never did say if he was cold the morning I woke up with his jacket over me. John, however, is clearly feeling the bite of the morning air.

There isn't a lot of preparation to be done. We have to make sure the fire is thoroughly extinguished, erase our tracks and pack our few bits of gear back into the bags. The sky is just beginning to color when we head out.

So far, the werewolves have not moved any further away. I'm still not sure if that's a good thing or not. With great effort, I push all other thoughts from my mind and try to focus only on the twin pulls of Elias and Zev. *Please let Langley be right*, I silently beg the surrounding forest.

We need to stop several times for Langley's sake. I'm grateful to have his experienced mind with us, but I'm also peeved that he's slowing us down. By almost midday we make it back to the cave. Even with Langley needing extra rest stops, we've made better time than when we were fleeing, and he needed to be carried. That's a little encouraging, I suppose.

We enter the camp cautiously in case anyone hung back to await our return. There are several bodies lying about, evidence of the fight Zev and Eli put up. Otherwise, the camp is completely deserted.

"Let's stop here for lunch," Langley says.

"Ugh! Near the dead bodies?" Sierra asks, making a face of disgust. For once, we agree. There's an entire forest out there I'd rather eat in.

Langley sits heavily on the ground and expels an exhausted breath. "Yes, near the bodies." I stow any arguments I had prepared. It's clear he's in need of an extended rest.

"Are you sure you should be heading to this battle?" John asks, his eyes full of concern.

"I'm fine," Langley all but snaps. John puts his hands up in surrender and retreats to a rock to eat his lunch.

There isn't much food with us. John had brought back some small game and cooked it yesterday. Thanks to the mountain's cool air, it should hold for a day or two, but there's probably only enough for today. None of us push to get going once we're done, waiting on Langley's signal to head out.

He dozes for a time. Still, the werewolves haven't moved, yet somehow, I sense our time is running out. It's my nerves, I'm sure. I'm jittery and on edge and I can't seem to sit still for more than a handful of seconds.

Finally, he hauls himself to his feet and ushers us onward. Some of the color has returned to his face, but he still seems weak. He should have listened and gone back.

For the number of people who tramped through here, there's surprisingly few signs of their passing. I'm only just realizing that they left such a clear trail for Zev and me so they could lure us in. If it wasn't for this weird homing system I have going on, we'd probably never find our friends. As it is, I have to stop frequently and test my connection. As far as my gut is concerned, we're headed in the right direction. Slowly but surely, the distance between us is closing.

The sun is almost gone when Langley announces it's time to stop. I bite back my comments. We're so close now, I can almost taste it. It would be ill advised to attack a pack of werewolves after dark, however, and we run the risk of being smelled or heard if we get too much closer. Resisting the urge to stomp my foot like a disgruntled child, I eat my evening ration and settle down for some sleep.

I'm awake again before the sun and quickly wake the others. Langley seems stronger today. I take heart from that. If nothing else, it would be nice if he can at least defend himself.

The sky has settled into a chilly gray color, threatening us with more snow, by the time we find the werewolves' new hideout. We stop and exchange shocked looks. Sprawled before us is a small village. Only Langley seems to take this in stride.

"I should have known they'd bring them here," he comments.

No one seems to be outside right now. Perhaps it's still too early for them to be awake. Or maybe they're lying in wait. I shudder at the thought.

"Can you sense them?" Langley whispers right in my ear. I nod. "Let's get this over with, then. Lead the way, quietly."

I swallow my fear and lead the way out of the trees and to the nearest building. Staying low and moving swiftly, we dodge from shadow to shadow until I stop us beside a building. "They're here," I whisper to Langley.

He glances at the building. It looks just like any other building here, made of oiled logs, one story tall, and square. Different from the others, however, is the trapdoor leading underground like a cellar entrance.

Tony tries to open it, only to find it locked. "So, now what?" he asks lamely.

"John?" Langley asks, giving his companion an expectant look.

John steps forward to examine the lock and door. "I'll need a few minutes, but I think I can get us in," he says thoughtfully.

"Make it one," Langley answers.

John pulls out a set of professional looking lock picks from an inner jacket pocket and gets to work on the lock. The rest of us wait impatiently, casting furtive glances at the surrounding buildings and shifting our weight from one foot to the other. It feels like an eternity, though it only takes him maybe ninety seconds, and then there's an audible clicking sound as the lock gives. He stands and gives the door a tug. It opens, its hinges squeaking slightly.

In pairs of two, weapons at the ready, we make our way down into the cellar. Sierra refuses to descend the stairs, so Tony hangs back with her to keep watch.

Tucked in a corner just outside the light pooling at the base of the stairs sits Elias, watching our arrival. Beside him, tied and unconscious, lies Zev. My heart skips in my throat as my stomach drops to the floor. We're too late to help him.

Kalia and Langley burst forward while I stand stupidly on the steps trying to process what I'm seeing. Zev can't be dead. I should be the one lying there so very still.

The first thing Kalia does is take Elias's head between her hands and plant a kiss on his mouth. She pulls back so they can touch their foreheads. "I was so afraid we'd be too late," she whispers.

Langley is on his knees beside Zev, trying to rouse him, his voice panicked. John and I stay back, tears threatening to escape my eyes. I'm relieved and terrified all at once. Eli is alive and whole, but Zev still hasn't moved.

"John, help me," Langley orders in a tight voice. John leaps forward to lend whatever assistance he can.

Kalia has Eli untied now. He's rubbing his wrists when our eyes meet, and I know he's reading every emotion tumbling inside of me. Pain, fear, relief, and a misplaced feeling of abandonment. I should've been the first one at his side, but Kalia had stolen that right. Part of me wants to go to Zev, but it wouldn't matter. Not to him.

"Minny?" Eli asks quietly. He still can't handle my meltdowns.

My tears break free and roll down my face. Eli holds out an arm to me and I stumble into his embrace. "I'm sorry," I choke out. "I thought... I can't... I was so scared I was going to lose you too."

"I know. I'm fine," he murmurs.

I pull away to look at Zev. "He's hurt because of me." John and Langley have Zev on his stomach while John does his best to doctor the knife wounds.

Langley looks up at my admission. His eyes are gentle and understanding as he reaches out to grip my hand. "Don't blame yourself. He made the choice to protect you."

At that moment, Zev stirs some. My heart does a somersault as he shifts and scrunches his face against the pain. Then his eyes blink open. "Langley?" He asks in a quiet voice.

Langley blinks back tears of his own as he runs a hand over Zev's hair in a fatherly gesture. "I'm right here, buddy."

Zev waves John away and shoves himself up into a sitting position, letting out a low hiss of pain. Langley sets to work cutting his ropes while he takes in the faces around him. His eyes settle on me. "You're crying," he says bluntly.

"Yeah," I answer, a smile starting to spread across my face.

He glances at Eli and then his eyes drop to where Eli's arm still rests around my waist. A cold look creeps into his eyes just before he looks away. "I told you we'd get your boyfriend back. You can stop crying now."

Eli pulls his arm away like he's been burned. "She's not my girlfriend," he says through gritted teeth. Zev just looks down at his hands and shrugs, then grimaces at the pain the motion causes.

"Never mind that. This isn't the time for you to be arguing. We need to go," Langley tells them. "Can you walk?" He asks Zev. Zev just nods and attempts to get to his feet.

He grunts and sits back once more. Langley offers a hand and with the help of him and John, Zev finds his feet. We're almost up the stairs when I sense them.

"We're too late," I say mostly to myself just before Tony appears.

"We've got company." He announces.

I draw my pistols. "You sure they're loaded?" Zev asks dryly. I glance back to see a glimmer of humor light his eyes in his otherwise humorless expression.

"Shut up," I answer. I wonder if he'll ever let me live that down.

As we step outside, we're greeted by a group of werewolves. Heading them is a man around Langley's age. His eyes are the same deep blue as Eli's, Zev's and Arya's. Scars riddle his face and arms, which are bare despite the cold weather. He smiles coldly at our ragtag group.

"Where do you think you're taking my sons?"

CHAPTER 15

Langley narrows his eyes at the werewolf. "I'm taking *my* sons home," he answers defiantly.

The man chuckles humorlessly. "You're a cocky one, aren't you? I don't recall having fought you for the right to claim them as yours."

"Father, he..." His hand flies out to smack Arya, standing just behind him, so fast that I almost miss it. She clutches her bruised face and stares at her feet, huddling within herself. She looks so pitiful I *almost* feel sorry for her.

"Shut up, useless welp!" He snaps. Beside me, Zev gives a low growl of warning.

"If you want my boys, you'll have to fight me for them," the man says, all traces of humor gone from his face.

Langley sizes him up in a glance. With his injuries still barely beginning to heal he doesn't stand a chance against the werewolf, and I think he realizes this. "Why don't you just let them go?" He suggests. "You want them dead, anyway, so just let me take them home. They won't bother you and you don't have to kill your own kin."

"That's not our way here. If you're too frightened to fight, then just walk away. Let me deal with my children as I see fit."

Langley bares his teeth and draws his blade. "No," he growls out.

"Father, maybe you should..." The man turns and grabs Arya by the throat, his claw like nails digging in until they draw blood. Zev lunges forward with a snarl only to be stopped by Langley's arm across his chest.

"Let her go," he demands in a growl. I hadn't expected such a reaction from him on Arya's behalf. Their last meeting didn't seem exactly friendly.

"She will hold her tongue or I will remove it." His father growls back. Arya's eyes meet Zev's, full of fear and pleading for help, as she struggles with her father's hand.

"Put her down, Mingan," Langley speaks up, keeping his tone even, "your fight isn't with her."

Mingan glares at our group, glances back at his daughter, and then tosses her aside like old trash. She hits the ground hard, rolling some before coming to a stop and curling into the fetal position. Zev growls again, Langley still keeping him from reaching his sister.

"Let's fight then," Mingan says.

Zev shoves Langley's arm aside and steps in front of him. "You're in no condition to fight him," he says over his shoulder. "Let me handle it."

Langley opens his mouth to argue, but Eli beats him to it. "Because your condition is so much better?" He smiles cockily. "Don't worry, big brother, I'll handle Daddy dearest." He steps forward, shaking free of Kalia's grasp, but Mingan only sneers. The werewolves behind him shift uneasily.

"That is not our way around here, boy. If Langley wants you, he must be the one to fight."

"That's nice," Eli answers nonchalantly, "but I'd rather claim myself."

Mingan chuckles. "You will fail." In an instant, his claws and teeth grow longer and hair sprouts over his body until he is a man in wolf form. Just as quickly, Eli sheds his own human form and charges his father. He never clears the distance between them, however.

Before he's gone two paces, Zev shoves him aside. Shifting forms as he goes, he throws his full weight into Mingan. Taken by surprise, Mingan goes down with Zev on top.

The other werewolves are urged into action at the sight of their alpha tangling with his son. Before we really know what's happening, we're set upon by the two dozen or so werewolves backing Mingan.

We're not well armed, but we're an aggressive bunch. We meet our challengers with a gusto, thrusting into them with our meager weapons. Even Kalia has set aside her usual sweet demeanor in order to push them back.

I'm surprised to find we have a second full blood werewolf fighting on our side. Diving into the fray at Eli's side is Arya. I don't know what to make of her sudden team change and right now I don't have time to contemplate it.

Tony goes down trying to defend Sierra. She screeches like a banshee as she plunges her dagger into the werewolves back before it can deliver the killing blow. On the other side, John is holding his own despite the claw marks tracking across his chest.

Langley staggers some, catches himself, and fights on doggedly. He's gone terribly pale from the exertion and sweat drips from his face. On his side, blood has begun to seep through his shirt where his wound had reopened.

My moment of distraction costs me. Claws rake their way across my side. I gasp in pain and whirl to meet my attacker only to have Eli plow him away. Instantly there's another to take his place. A quick, bright eyed female. She is quickly dispatched with a swift dodge and a thrust of my spear.

I turn to meet whoever's coming next and see Arya go down. They've teamed up on her for her betrayal of the pack. I should let them have her after she tried feeding me to them, but my feet are already moving to help. I start wading through them when Zev charges in on the other side. He tears into them like they're nothing, digging his way to his twin. I continue pressing my way towards her also, though the werewolves hardly seem to notice me. Most of their focus is on the two siblings battling them.

I wonder, briefly, if Mingan is dead since Zev is now fighting this battle. We reach Arya at the same time, each of us taking an arm to hoist her to her feet. At that moment, a snarling mass of fur barrels into Zev. I guess Mingan's not dead yet, unfortunately. All around us, the rest of the fight is dying down as the werewolves stop to watch the outcome of the fight between father and son.

Zev's strength is failing, and his back wounds are bleeding again along with many new injuries. I see him slip and my feet are moving before my mind's caught up, fear driving me forward. Another blow and Zev hits the ground, barely conscious.

Mingan rears back to deliver the killing blow only to find my gun aimed directly at his head. An icy calm floods through me as I glare at him across Zev's prone form. "I advise you to step away," I tell him in a low, warning voice. His lips draw back in a doglike smile. The set of his head says he doesn't believe I'll do it. I pull back the hammer. "I will not allow you to murder any more of my family," I growl.

His smile falters slightly. Behind me, Eli and Arya step up to flank me. He eyes all of us as though taking our measure, snarls ferociously, and draws back to strike. The sound of a double shot fills the air, and he freezes, his eyes wide in shock.

Slowly, he returns to human form, sinking to his knees. His eyes glaze over and he lurches onto his side. Behind him stands Langley, my other pistol held between both his hands. We'd fired at the same time.

At my feet, Zev has also returned to human form. I drop to my knees beside him and roll him onto his back as Langley hurries over. All my calm has rushed away to be replaced with the cold grip of fear once more. He can't be gone, not now. Not after everything we've gone through. Not so soon after getting him back.

He grimaces at the feeling of being turned, and I gasp in relief. "Thank the ancestors," I whisper, suppressing the urge to throw myself at him.

He blinks his eyes open and looks from me to Langley. "Did I win?" Langley and I both chuckle at that.

Langley shakes his head leaning down to help Zev into a sitting position. "No, sorry, Zev. You'll have to thank Amane for Mingan's end."

"Why would *you* kill him?"

I shrug. "I guess I was just done letting him kill the people I care about. Purely selfish really."

He smiles, that beautiful smile that lights up his whole face. "By all means, be selfish more often."

I smile back. "Or you could just stop almost dying every time I turn around."

His smile fades suddenly as he glances at all the werewolves surrounding us and then looks back at me. "You realize you're their alpha now?"

I can feel the color leave my face. "No, not me. You can do it."

"He can't." Arya joins us on her knees. It strikes me suddenly how completely comfortable they are about the fact that they're totally naked.

"Sure, he can," I insist desperately. "I'm passing the crown."

"You can't. That's not how it works," she says. "But... Langley can." I give her a puzzled look. How can Langley pass on a crown that isn't his?

"Langley also shot Mingan. It may not have been the killing shot, but sometimes such lines can be blurred. Langley can claim the pack as his own and pass the mantle to either of his sons. Or the boys can fight you to the death for it."

I meet Zev's eyes, but his look says it's up to me. I look back to Arya. "What about you? Couldn't Langley give the pack to you?"

She shakes her head. "Females cannot inherit their packs unless they kill the alpha, like you did. It can only pass to males."

Langley and Zev share a look. "Some traditions need to be revised sometimes," Langley says. "I would like to pass the leadership of my pack to the sister of my sons as I am unfit for the position and I believe both boys have pursuits they would like to follow."

I glance back at Eli, now human again, to see his reaction. Kalia slips her hand into his and they share a smile. I guess that answers that question.

Arya smiles widely, revealing all of her teeth. "Really?" She looks at Zev. "Are you sure?"

He nods at his sister. "I have too many memories of these mountains I'd rather leave in the past. I have no desire to dwell in them."

Langley nods and stands. "As the male who has defeated your alpha, I now pass that honor to the closest of my kin willing to lead you, Arya Lycidas." There's some shifting and unease in the group. "If you have any objections, I am willing to fight them out," he tells them. The shifting settles into grudging acceptance.

"Can we get out of here, now?" Sierra asks.

Langley surveys our group. "We'll need a day or two. Most of us need medical attention first." Sierra lets out a groan, and Tony rubs her back reassuringly.

Arya stands and begins issuing orders to her pack. The injured are gathered and moved into a building hastily set up as an infirmary. Together, John and Elias get Zev inside, his adrenaline having faded enough for the full extent of his injuries to register.

It's not good. He's lost a lot of blood and he's riddled with claw and bite marks now. Thankfully, there's a physician in the village. An old healer who hung back from the fighting due to age and the knowledge that she would be needed when the fighting stopped.

She does a wonderful job patching up Arya, Zev and Eli, but she's more reluctant to treat the rest of us. For the most part we take care of each other, field dress being a rudimentary part of training. Langley needs more attention than we can provide, however. The fact that he's still functioning at all is a testament to his sheer force of will. As soon as the rest of us are treated, John insists he lay down and be treated. Arya reinforces this when she berates the old, prejudice physician.

CHAPTER 16

Sunset finds Arya, Elias and I gathered around Zev and Langley's sickbeds. Arya sits cross-legged at Zev's feet while Eli takes a seat in a chair he dragged over. I'm standing beside him, listening to their banter.

There's a comfortable warmth here, even though they only just realized their connection to one another. The four of them are a family, damaged by their pasts and twisted together at odd angles, but still a family. A whisper of a smile crosses my lips as happiness fills my heart for Eli. It's not his mother, but it's everything she ever wanted for him.

Feeling my presence is unnecessary and my role as sister has reached its end, I begin exiting slowly. I edge towards the end of the bed before Eli reaches out and grabs my hand. "Where are you going?" He asks.

"I… Uh…" I stutter. "I just thought you'd want some time with your family."

He grins. "You're over-thinking again, Minny. How can I possibly enjoy family time when part of it has wandered off?"

I blink at him and glance sideways at Arya. "But I…"

He interrupts, having seen my look. "Arya's not replacing you, you goon. Now I have two sisters."

Arya flashes a smile. "I always wanted a little sister."

That's a strange response, considering she tried to feed me to her pack just days ago. The sentiment warms me just the same, however. I glance at Zev to see where he stands on this matter, but he's working hard at appearing completely absorbed in examining his hands.

Arya takes my other hand and drags me down beside her. "Come, sit, stay with us for a while," she insists. She doesn't leave me much of a choice.

They resume their conversation and I sit back to listen. I chance another glance at Zev. This time his eyes lock onto mine for a minute and I can't seem to look away. I don't think he's pleased with his sibling's decision. A door closes and I blink at the sound, breaking the spell. I look away quickly, becoming enthralled in my own hands.

Kalia strides up between the rows of beds to join us. She hesitates at the foot of the bed. "Sorry, am I interrupting something?" She asks.

"No, not at all." Eli answers, holding out an arm to her. She smiles and steps into it. He pulls her onto his lap and kisses her before looking at his brother. "So you're no longer confused on the matter. This is my girlfriend." Then he points a finger from me to Kalia. "Sister. Girlfriend. 'Kay?" Zev simply scowls his answer, which causes Langley and Arya to chuckle.

Those of our team not bed ridden are ushered into a tiny, hut style house near the infirmary. There are no comforts here, but at least it's inside and, for the first time in a week, we don't have to sleep on top of snow. It doesn't escape my notice that Sierra finds a spot near Tony to bed down. She seems to be the only one who didn't sustain any injuries and I'm convinced it's because of her unfiltered disgust at the very notion of being touched by a werewolf. I wonder how desperately she wanted to shower after learning of Eli's heritage.

My instincts wake me more than the creak of the door opening. My eyes open to the room still being pitch black, and then Zev's in front of me. "Good, you're up," he whispers. "I want to show you something."

"As nice as they look in their natural habitat, I'm going to be seriously peeved if you're waking me before the sun to look at deer again," I whisper back as I climb to my feet, careful not to jostle Kalia. She, Eli, and I had fallen asleep in a small huddle. She's probably the warmest person in here being squished between the two of us.

I follow Zev's dark outline out into the cold, mountain morning. Instantly, a shiver runs through me, reminding me that I forgot my jacket inside. Zev strips off his own and drapes it over my shoulders. "This way," he urges, leading me into the trees.

I follow him for about a quarter of a mile, the sky beginning to gray before complaining. "Seriously, Zev, where are you taking me?"

"We're almost there, just come," he answers without looking back.

"You shouldn't even be out of bed in your condition," I grumble at his back. I know he can hear me, but he doesn't reply.

Soon, the trees start to thin, and the world looks like it falls away ahead of us. Zev stops right on the edge, and I come up alongside him. From here, it feels like you can see everything. Down below, you can see where the trees peter out and a small town begins. The view stretches for miles beyond that.

"Woah!" I breathe. He smiles in satisfaction. "Tell me again why you couldn't show me this after the sun was up?"

He simply points at the horizon, where a faint bit of yellow is starting to touch the sky. "You brought me here to watch the sunrise?" I ask, slightly shocked.

"You can't get a better view," he answers, sitting down to watch the show. Zev is a complicated person.

I sit beside him and huddle inside the jacket. There's a bit of a breeze up here, but the jacket blocks most of it out. We sit in comfortable silence as the sky shifts into colors of purple, pink and red.

"Why did you pick up the journals?" I ask.

He's quiet for so long I begin to wonder if he's going to answer. "I thought... Maybe you'd want to send them away differently. You know... Instead of leaving them in the woods."

I think about it for a minute and realize he's right. "I want to burn them. I think that's fitting." He gives me an assessing look before nodding.

And then he asks the one question I have yet to find an answer for. "Where are you planning to go when we get back?"

"I don't know," I answer with a shake of my head.

"Will you go home?"

I clear my throat. "I don't actually have a home anymore." Seeing the question in his eyes, I elaborate. "We burned it down with our parents' bodies inside to hide the werewolf wounds on them. Eli tried to make it look like an accident. A bonfire party gone wrong."

"So, you have nothing? Those journals, they really are... Everything?"

I smile then, trying to push away the grief I've been fighting this entire journey. "I have Elias, so I have everything I need."

He digests this. "When you said he was your family, you meant..."

"That my family begins and ends with him."

"And now?"

A chuckle bubbles in my chest. "Apparently, I have a big sister now, a surrogate father, and real friends. Who knew we'd have to lose our family to find our family?"

By now, the sky has settled into a cloudless blue. Without a word or even looking at me, Zev reaches over and entwines his fingers with mine, giving my hand a gentle squeeze. I notice he still doesn't claim me as a sister the way his siblings did. Just friends then. I squeeze back, grateful for the quiet support.

"Do you think Arya will try feeding me to the pack again?" I'm only partly joking.

He growls at the memory. "She better not."

On a more serious note, I ask, "why do you think she switched sides so suddenly?"

"She didn't. She's always been on our side, but she needed to put on a good show to keep Mingan from killing her. He only ever kept her alive to use against me." His eyes flick over me. "She *was* going to let them eat you, though, whether she really wanted to or not. She really did want to hurt Elias and me. She blamed us for the torment she received at Mingan's hands."

"And now?"

He shrugs, looking at the view. "She's free of him, and she's forgiven us." As though they've done anything that needed to be forgiven. I can see on Zev's face that he still feels guilty, however.

"Whatever he did to her, it wasn't your fault," I tell him.

"I've known for years that she was here. I knew Langley was looking for her and I never said anything. She told me not to, but I should have. She could have been safe."

I don't know how to respond to that. It's going to take a long time before he forgives himself, I know that much. I give his hand another squeeze and look back at the view.

After maybe another twenty minutes, he rises, pulling me up beside him. "Langley's going to kill me when he sees me out of bed." He releases my hand and leads me back through the trees.

"Can I ask you a sensitive question?" I ask. When he answers with silence, I press on. "Langley said he found you in a cage. He didn't say how he got you away from an entire pack of werewolves, though."

"He fought them."

I stop in shock. "All of them?"

"It's the only way he could claim the rights to me." No wonder Zev's so loyal to Langley, besides the obvious love Langley has for him. Langley's a serious badass! Then again, you'd have to be a badass to pursue a relationship with a woman as intense as Dorris and willingly raise a werewolf child.

"Did they give you your scar, or did that come from the field?" No answer. I can almost feel him shutting me out again. I want to demand an answer. Anything to keep him from shutting me out, but it's not my place. "Sorry," I mumble.

He slows to a stop, and I stop behind him. "I don't like to remember that day." He says without turning, his fists clenching at his sides. "I wish I could forget, but I'm reminded every time I look in a mirror. And when I'm not seeing it, there's always someone to point it out."

"I'm sorry. I didn't mean to remind you. Forget I asked." Guilt floods through me.

"No," he answers, a harsh edge to his voice. "You asked because that's what you see when you look at me." Beneath the edge there's a bit of hurt in his voice. The sound of a boy who's only ever been noticed for his disfigurement.

I shrug, aiming for nonchalance. "I mean, it's a part of your face, so it's hard to miss, but it's not what draws the eye."

Now he does turn to look at me, startled. "What?"

I smile brightly at him. "Your eyes are different colors. I assume it's because you were blinded in your right one when you got your scar, but they're definitely an eye catcher. I guess that's really why I asked. I was just curious about how long you've been half blind." I think about that momentarily, my smile fading. "I suppose I should have asked differently."

The fight has gone out of him now, though he still looks confused, like I'm the one that doesn't make sense. "Since I was eight." He sighs, glances away, and then unexpectedly and totally out of character for him, he elaborates. "I was used in death matches back then. That's how they were training me to fight Mingan. Always against other children, and I always won."

"Clearly," I say before clapping both hands over my mouth. That was incredibly insensitive.

He doesn't react at all, plowing ahead. "The boy was also eight. He was tall for our age, with unkempt, brown hair and wild eyes. A sprinkling of freckles. We fought in wolf form. He caught me with a claw, and I ripped out his throat. Them or me, that simple. I chose me, over and over and over."

He turns abruptly, apparently done with his story. I catch him mid-step, wrapping my arms around his waist and holding him to me, trying to convey how sincerely sorry I am that he had to go through that. I feel his tension melt away as he places his hands over my arms.

"We should get back," he says. I release him and we continue back to the village.

Langley opens his mouth to scold Zev as soon as we enter the building, takes one look at his face, and switches gears. "What's wrong? What happened?" He's gone into full concerned parent mode. Zev just shakes his head and Langley looks at me. "What happened?" He repeats.

I glance at Zev as he climbs back into bed facing away from me. "I pushed on a wall I should have left alone," I answer honestly, not hiding the regret I feel for causing him pain. "I should get back to the others." I leave before Langley can interrogate me further.

An hour later, he finds me sitting under a tree. "You shouldn't be up," I tell him.

"I need to talk to you." He dismisses my scolding as he slides onto the ground beside me.

"Does Zev know you're up?"

"He's sleeping."

"Oh." That's a good thing. He definitely needs the rest.

Langley stares at me until I'm forced to meet his eyes. "What did he tell you?" He asks.

I look away and stab at the ground with a stick. "Nothing," I mumble. I am a truly terrible liar. I can keep secrets no problem but ask me about something point blank and I cave like a snow fort in Spring.

"Amane, look at me." Not wanting to be the first to disobey an order from Langley, I do as he says. "I'm not upset. It's his right to share his thoughts and feelings as he chooses. But it's my right to know why he looked so utterly defeated when he returned this morning. Please, what did he tell you?"

"He told me about the death matches. I didn't mean to pry. I didn't know. I just wanted to know how long he's been blind in his right eye. I asked the wrong question. I never meant to hurt him," I spew all of this in a rush of words.

Langley sits back and lets out a slow breath. "That's... A huge step for him. He's barely mentioned those days, even to me. What did you ask that prompted him to tell you?"

"I just asked when he got the scar. Then he went on a rant about how that's all people see. Well, as much of a rant as I think Zev is capable of. I apologized and explained that I was really asking about his eye and not necessarily the scar and then he just... Decided to tell me, I guess."

His eyes narrow at me. "You said you pushed."

I look away and poke the ground some more. "It sure felt like pushing."

"But it wasn't. He just... Decided to tell you." I can feel Langley studying me like I'm some kind of new species.

"If he decided without me pushing, then why did he look like I whipped him?" I'm angry, but I'm not sure why. Mostly at myself I believe.

"Those memories are very painful for him. He pushes them down, ignores them, pretends they belong to someone else. All things I'm certain a psychiatrist would frown upon. Since he's never allowed himself to really look at them or work through the emotions tied to them, he's never really healed from them. So, when he made the choice to share them with you, well, he had to see them, to feel them. It wasn't something you did. It's just something he needs to work through."

I stop poking at the ground and just stare at the holes. I still feel incredibly guilty about having made him think about those memories. "I didn't mean to hurt him. I would never hurt him on purpose."

Langley places a hand on my head. "He knows that, Amane. It's for that very reason that he trusts you the way he does." He climbs to his feet, gritting his teeth against the pain of the movement. "Zev doesn't trust easily, believe me on that." Our conversation at an end, he carefully makes his way back to the infirmary. Hopefully, he manages to get some more rest.

I spend the better part of the day avoiding the infirmary, using my time to restock our supplies. There's a pyre set up for burning the bodies of those who didn't survive the fight. A small group of mourners gather to watch.

When I'm done gathering supplies, I join them. I didn't really know Mingan and what I did know, I hated. He took everything from me, but he's also the reason I have a family now. I believe that's a good enough reason to pay my respects.

Watching the flames leaping for the sky and hungrily devouring the wood and flesh provided to feed it sends me back to that awful night just over a week past. The screams, the snarls, the flames, the fear. I close my eyes and turn away, pushing the memories down. I'm not ready to face them yet. Not here.

I've been suppressing the memories and the pain they inevitably bring since Elias and I hit the road. More than once I've thought to tell Mom or Dad about the things that we've experienced on this mission only for the memory that they're gone to crash into me like a sledgehammer. It always comes as a shock that I won't see them again or talk to them again. Then I breathe and think about anything else, force myself to forget again for a while. Luckily, we've been busy since that night, so distractions aren't hard to come by. Today, a new fear has surfaced, however. What's going to distract me when this is all over?

I breathe and square my shoulders, hardening myself against the mental flood once again. I need something to do. Anything to busy my mind. Maybe I should find Elias. Where *is* he, anyhow?

Following my instincts leads me into the trees. I find him sitting alone on a boulder and staring into the woods. I climb up beside him and dangle my legs over the edge. "Something wrong, Atlas?"

He glances at me, a half-smile tugging at the corner of his mouth. "I was just thinking, what happens now? Where do we go?"

"*We?*" I ask. I hadn't thought he and I were a 'we' anymore. Not in the same sense we used to be.

He bumps his shoulder against me. "Yeah, you and me, Minny. Us against the world, just like always."

"What about Kalia?"

His smile blossoms fully now and for the first time I see a true resemblance between him and Zev. "Maybe our 'we' has grown a bit, but we're still the core of it."

I let that sink in. A bigger 'we', starting with us and blossoming outward. The idea has a kind of beauty to it, and a reassurance. Whatever the world throws at us, whoever comes and goes through our lives, there will always be Eli and me.

"You still have your mom's place," I say.

"True." He nods. "We could go back there if you wanted to."

"Do *you* want to?"

He considers that and shrugs. "I don't feel like there's a lot left for us there without our parents. I'll go, though, if that's what you want."

He's right. Neither of us really expanded our friend group beyond each other. We spent all of our extra free time training or playing in the woods away from the world. There's no one there who would miss us. I shake my head. "I don't want to go back."

"Do you think the hunters would take us?" He asks speculatively.

"I think so. Our parents seem to have been something of a legend with them. I think we'd have a foot in the door even without as much training as we've had." I wonder if Benjamin will be willing to overlook Eli's werewolf blood in favor of having a skilled hunter in his force.

"What do you think? Want to do it?"

I think it over before replying. "Maybe, if they have a job that requires less killing."

His smile returns. "Maybe they have a werewolf relations department. They could send you to sign peace treaties and such."

I chuckle at the thought. "Perhaps."

A crunching sound behind us draws our attention. We turn to see Arya watching us. "Is this a private meeting?" She asks.

"Just trying to plan our future now that we don't have a past to return to." Eli answers.

Arya raises an eyebrow. "Intriguing. In fair warning, most werewolves don't appreciate others sneaking off with their mates. So, maybe don't mention this little rendezvous to Zev."

It takes a minute for her words to sink in, and then I roll my eyes. "I am *not* Zev's mate!"

She tilts her head slightly like she's thinking over my argument, and then shrugs. "I still think you're lying. You don't have to, you know. I promise not to try feeding you to the pack again."

"Well, thanks. I appreciate the sentiment, but I'm still not his mate. We're just friends… I think. Or maybe just two people headed in the same direction? You know, I'm not really sure what exactly the nature of our relationship is." I certainly care for him as more than just a passing acquaintance, but I'm not sure we could be classified as friends. Nor am I certain he wants anything more from our relationship than a passing acquaintance.

Arya seems less than interested in my current confusion. "Well, in that case, I only called you sister because I still assumed you and Zev were actually a thing." I think I may be a little disappointed about that. It was a cool idea to believe I had a sister for that short period of time.

She smiles suddenly. "But you did help save me from my own pack and you put that bullet in Mingan, so I guess that counts for something. Plus, I really have always wanted a sister. Zev's great as far as twins go, but you can't have a decent girl talk with your brother."

I smile back. "You can say that again."

Eli makes a face. "Hey, I tried." I give his shoulder a consoling pat.

"Anyhow, Langley sent me to find you two. He wants to double check that everything's ready for your departure tomorrow," Arya announces.

"Do you really think he'll be ready to go tomorrow?" I ask her.

She shrugs again. "No, but do *you* want to be the one to tell him no?"

I shake my head. "No, you're right. Never mind."

No longer able to avoid the infirmary and facing Zev, I follow Elias and Arya back. Zev and Langley are both sitting up and facing each other. John is leaning against the wall between the beds while Sierra sits beside Langley and Tony stands at the foot of his bed. Kalia is standing at the foot of Zev's bed.

Arya climbs up beside her twin, loops her arm through his and rests her head on his shoulder. Eli puts an arm around Kalia's waist, and she leans into him. I take up a spot sort of awkwardly between him and Tony. The gang's all here.

"Alright, now that we're all here, how are preparations going for tomorrow's departure?" Langley starts right in.

"Tony and I have seen to our weapon supply. Arya's been kind enough to lend us a couple of spears and even a gun." John says.

"Will they be necessary?" Sierra asks. "Aren't we on good terms now?"

"Mine is not the only pack in these mountains." Arya explains. "And the others may be less amicable to hunters being here."

Langley nods his agreement. "And the other supplies?"

"I've gathered several canteens of water and some food." I answer. "But since we're down to just the two packs, there isn't much space."

"Is there anything we can leave behind to make additional space?" He asks.

Most of what's in them is gear that may prove useful, but my parents' journals could stay. Food is probably more important. The group is watching as I do a mental inventory. "Yes." I answer in the same instant Zev says, "no."

Our eyes meet, and a silent battle of the wills follows. After a moment, I look away, cross my arms, and sigh. "We've already paired down to the bare minimum." Zev tells Langley. "What's left should stay."

"All right," Langley says. "We'll make do with what we've got. Hopefully, we can retrieve the rest of our gear on the way down."

Eli and Arya exchange looks. "Are we just going to pretend that stare down didn't happen?" Eli asks.

Langley shrugs. "Seemed like a private matter. Now, everyone out so we can get a little more healing done."

Without meeting anyone else's eyes, I turn on my heel and leave. I am grateful that Zev's fighting for my right to hold on to the journals until a time when I can properly part with them. However, given the circumstances, I believe we'd be better off leaving them behind.

Elias catches up with me and paces at my side. "What was that about?" He asks.

"What?" I try acting nonchalant.

He gives me a look that says I'm not fooling anyone. "What were you and Zev arguing about?"

"We weren't arguing," I deflect.

"Not verbally, but if you'll recall, I have already had a similar silent argument with him."

I heave a sigh. "Alright, fine. Both of my parents' journals are in Zev's bag. They were completely ruined when I fell in the lake and I was just going to leave them in the woods, but he won't let me. He wants me to be able to get rid of them in a way that will, I don't know, bring me closure or something."

Eli lets that roll around in his brain some and then shrugs. "I don't understand why that's pissing you off. It seems awfully sweet to me. Especially coming from him."

"It just seems silly to haul two useless books around a mountain when it cuts into the food supply for everyone else."

"Don't worry about the food supply. Zev and I can both hunt for any food we may run short on. Bring the books."

"Fine," I grumble. "You're supposed to be on my side, though."

He chuckles at that. "I'm always on your side, Minny. I'm just thinking of the long game here. You don't want to become a bitter old grump before your twenties like my dear, big brother, do you?"

"I guess not," I answer with a smile.

He becomes serious again. "Speaking of the journals, I found something in your bag. I swear I wasn't rummaging around through your private things. I just needed something, and I stumbled on this." He pulls out Dad's letter to me.

I snatch it from his hand. "You weren't supposed to see that!" I hide it from view as though he hasn't already read it.

"It's fine. I guess, I always sort of thought maybe he didn't trust me," He says with a half-hearted smile.

"But...?" I know there's more he isn't saying.

"It still kind of hurts. I mean, he was the closest thing I had to a father. I used to go to him with my problems, things only guys can relate to. I always looked up to him, wanted to be just like him when I grew up. To know he didn't trust me with *you*. I don't care whose blood is in my veins, I would *never* hurt you."

I rest my hand on his shoulder, offering what comfort I can. "*I* know that, Eli. And I think Dad did too. He could just be a little overprotective sometimes, but he still loved you. I know that without any doubt."

123

He forces a smile. "Yeah, I know that. I just... I wish I would've known before. I wish..." He pauses to look away and clear his throat. "I wish I could have talked to him about it."

"Yeah," I agree, looking at the ground. "Yeah, I felt that too." Eli folds me into his arms and holds me tight without saying another word. When he draws a breath, I feel him shudder and I know he's crying quietly. I haven't seen him cry since that night and I know it's because he's been repressing it just as forcibly as I have. I tighten my grip just a little, enough to let him know I'm here.

After several minutes he takes another deep breath and pulls away to dry his face on a sleeve. I can feel the dampness on my shoulder from his tears. "Sorry." He won't meet my eyes, like he's ashamed of his emotions.

I smile weakly. "Don't apologize. It takes a strong person to confront their emotions head on." He meets my eyes now, and a small smile answers mine.

Kalia calls for him then. "How does my face look?" He asks, wiping it again. He's still not to a point where he wants her to know he cries, which is ridiculous. Everyone cries sometimes.

"Hideous," I answer with a grin.

He rolls his eyes. "I didn't ask about your reflection." I mock gasp and shove him. He chuckles. "Seriously, though, do I look like I've been crying?"

"Or you yawned really big."

"We'll go with that."

Kalia joins us and smiles brightly up at him until she sees his eyes. "Are you ok?" She asks, suddenly concerned. "Were you crying?"

"No, I'm fine. Just yawned is all." Elias has had a lot more practice lying that I have, which means he's way more convincing. He smiles at her. "What's up?"

She doesn't look quite convinced, but lets it go. "I thought we could take a walk. I hear there's a wonderful view about a quarter mile from here."

"Yes, it's breath taking," I supply.

Eli gives me a quizzical look. "When did you see it?"

I shrug, trying to seem casual about it. "Zev took me this morning. He wanted to show me the sunrise from there."

Eli seems like he wants to ask more about it, but Kalia just beams at me. "That's so sweet! I bet it looked amazing! What a romantic idea." She turns to Eli, buying me a moment to hide my blush. "Can we go, please?"

His questions forgotten in her pleading gaze, he smiles warmly. "Yeah, let's do it." He takes her hand to lead her away. "We'll be back before sunset," He tells me.

"Don't rush. I bet the sunset is just as lovely as the sunrise." I reply. He gives me a thumbs up and then they're gone.

Langley and Zev have us up before dawn. Arya meets us at the edge of the village to see us off. She embraces both Elias and I briefly, and even Langley. She stops before Zev and just looks at him for a long moment. A smile tugs at the corner of his mouth and he pulls her into his arms.

"Stay out of trouble," he tells her. "I can't spend all of my time freeing my little sister."

"We're the same age, you ass." She giggles.

Now he smiles for real as he releases her. "I have at least ten minutes on you."

She crosses her arms. "Well, girls mature faster, so I'm still older mentally."

He shrugs. "Whatever helps you sleep at night."

Her smile fades slightly and I think she might cry. She holds her hand out to him and he squeezes it gently. "Thank you. And I'm sorry. For everything. Don't be a stranger, alright?"

"Only if you stop apologizing," he tells her seriously.

"I'll try. I make no promises, though." She releases his hand and steps aside. "Be safe out there, Wolfie."

He scowls. "I hate that name."

She grins. "I know." With a final glance, he moves past her and we're off.

CHAPTER 17

The going is slow with us stopping at regular intervals for Zev and Langley to rest. Langley puts the stops to better use than Zev, who mostly paces during them. We take on the same procession we had when we came up the mountain. John and Langley on point, followed by Tony and Sierra, then Eli and Kalia, with me trailing and Zev taking the rear. Maybe I'm imagining things, but I get the distinct impression that he's avoiding me. Not that I'm doing any differently. I'm trying to respect his personal space, something I feel he probably needs quite a bit from me right now.

We reach the lake just after sunset and decide to stop for the night. I don't know what the others are planning, but I think I could forge a decent trail around the edge of the lake for myself. Sure, it may add about half a day to the journey, but better that than dying of hypothermia. I shudder at the memory and turn my back on the frozen body of water.

As though he's reading my thoughts, Zev turns to Langley. "We should skirt the lake tomorrow."

Langley looks from the lake to him. "Are you sure? It'll add at least half a day. It seemed sturdy enough when we came across a few days ago."

"I'm sure," Zev answers firmly.

Langley seems confused. "Zev, I thought we worked past that fear." Zev glances at me from the corner of his eye, but Langley catches the look. He takes in my clothes that aren't mine and the way I'm clearly avoiding looking at the water and realization dawns on his face. "We'll skirt it tomorrow. No need for unnecessary risks."

I breathe a sigh of relief. I hadn't even realized I was holding my breath. It's nice that Zev is looking out for me even if he is avoiding me right now.

"Zev's afraid of water?" Sierra asks in disbelief.

"No, he was once afraid of falling through the ice," Langley answers. "That was a long time ago, after a bad experience doing just that."

"Really? What happened?" Sierra leans forward, full of intrigue.

Langley blinks at her. "I just said he fell through the ice."

"But then what happened?" She presses. I try not to look overly interested, but it's a question Zev expertly avoided last time I asked.

"I helped pull him out and got his temperature stabilized again. Then I sent him back in, repeatedly, until he knew how to get himself out."

"That's so mean!" Kalia gasps.

He raises his eyebrows at her. "Was it? Zev, are you afraid of falling through the ice anymore?"

Zev shakes his head. "No, sir."

Kalia looks at me. "Didn't you fall through?" I nod. "Are you afraid?"

I shrug. "I certainly don't want to repeat the experience."

"So maybe we should send you in again so you're not afraid." Sierra suggests.

I start to argue, but Eli speaks up first. "Why don't we send you in?" She purses her lips and falls silent.

We alternate guard duty through the night, excluding Zev and Langley. It's a quiet night, the wind whispering across the lake and the waning moon providing just enough to see by. It's peaceful and inviting. When Eli rises to switch with me, I turn in reluctantly.

The morning light turns the ice a warm, pink color as we set out again. Spirits are high today after a good night's sleep and the coming promise of a warm day. There's constant teasing and a lightness to our steps that belies the arduous week that lies behind us.

At one point, Langley rolls his eyes and looks at John. "Remind me why I brought a bunch of kids."

John smiles at him. "Beats me. I've been questioning that since we left."

Only Zev seems extra broody as he brings up the rear. I don't sense any danger ahead, so I don't understand what's bugging him. I consider dropping back to ask, but I'm afraid of intruding where I'm not welcome. Elias has no such qualms, however.

He stops to wait for Zev and then falls into step beside him. "What's eating you today?" He asks.

Zev scowls without looking at him. "None of your business."

Eli grins. "Sure it is. Isn't that part of being family?" Zev doesn't answer. "Come on, we're brothers. You can tell me."

"You," Zev growls. "You're my problem."

"I haven't been near you all day," Eli remarks.

"And now you are, so currently, you're my problem." Spoken like a true big brother.

"Boys," Langley calls back, "don't make me separate you."

"Please do," answers Zev.

Kalia and I share a smile as Eli heaves a sigh. "Fine, don't tell me. Just sulk then." He walks ahead until he's beside me. "You could've warned me about brothers."

I shrug. "I could've, but you wouldn't have listened."

As the day moves towards dusk the mood begins to sober. I'm starting to feel that now familiar feeling in my gut that comes when there's danger ahead. I can tell by the set of Eli's back and the way he keeps scanning the tree line that he feels it too, and I assume Zev does as well. The others don't seem to notice anything.

I reach back to pull my box of bullets out of the side pocket of my bag and set about making sure both pistols are loaded. Behind me, I hear Zev close the distance between us until he's just a step or two back. Ahead, Elias checks his blades. The rest of our group continues their lighthearted banter.

A quarter of an hour later, Eli droops back once again. "What do you think?" He asks.

"We've probably got until dark. Maybe twenty minutes," I answer.

"We should alert the others," Zev says quietly.

Eli nods his agreement. "Should we stop here?"

"No," Zev answers. "Let the enemy believe we're clueless. It may give us an edge."

"Right," Eli agrees. He moves back up beside Kalia and whispers to her. She then moves up beside Sierra and Tony to pass along the news and Tony passes it up to John and Langley. We do our best to continue the conversations as though nothing's changed while also checking weapons and staying alert.

Slowly the sun slips down behind the trees and the moon begins to climb above the trees. I notice eyes reflecting the moonlight in my peripheral vision. "On the right," I murmur to Zev.

"Be ready," He whispers back. I hold my gun at my side, ready to react.

"We should make camp pretty soon," John remarks loud enough for us all to hear. "Probably not a good idea to wander around too much after dark."

"Let's find a clearing," Langley suggests.

A snarl comes from my right, and a beast launches out at us. My gun is up and a bullet flying before the thought consciously hits my brain. The werewolf freezes mid-step before crumpling to the ground and reverting to human form.

Suddenly we're surrounded by eight of them. Very fair odds, I must say. Zev turns so we're back-to-back and draws a dagger in each hand. The others take the same stance with the person beside them. All of this takes place in the span of several heartbeats.

These werewolves fight dirty. In the past, the ones attacking us have stuck strictly to claw use, seeming almost afraid to turn us. These ones have no issues gnashing their teeth at us and trying to land a bite. They also seem much stronger than our previous adversaries. I wonder what the difference is between them.

I have my spear out now as I try to gain some distance between myself and this new threat. Then I can draw my pistol again.

A werewolf lunges, teeth bared to bite me. I use the spear haft to deflect. Her jaws close around the wood and snap it in half. "Oh, shit!" The words squeak out of me without permission.

She continues her advancement and I back away, my mind racing for a new course of action. I draw my pistols, firing two rounds into her and she pauses. But doesn't stop.

I dodge her gnashing teeth again, throwing myself to the side, rolling, and coming to my feet in a crouch. My roll took me away from Zev and I feel that empty space at my back as a chill runs down my spine.

I'm barely up and she's on me again. I fire another two rounds and roll again. She should be down, but she's still coming like some kind of psychotic zombie werewolf. I know my bullets are finding marks, yet she's reacting as though they're nothing at all. She's moving too fast and too close for me to get a proper drop for a kill shot.

I'm about to shoot again when werewolf Zev slams into her, his jaws closing around her throat. They hit the ground and roll, a tangle of claws and flying fur. He rises on his hind legs when they come to a halt and a third werewolf tackles him.

In the trees ahead, Elias is fighting a similar battle while John and Langley have teamed up on the same beast. Sierra has a large wound in her shoulder where she's been bitten and Tony's trying to stop the bleeding. Kalia is valiantly trying to fend off the final werewolf, but she's losing ground fast.

"Kalia, duck!" I shout at her. Instantly, she drops, and I put three rounds into her opponent's head. This one actually falls and doesn't move again, returning to its human form. We turn our attention towards the fights being waged by Eli and Zev. John and Langley seem to have their own battle under control.

I can't get a clear shot at either of the two fighting Zev, but one of Eli's has backed away to catch its breath. She's bleeding from a dozen wounds, none of them fatal. I place two bullets in her head and one in her chest.

In those few seconds, Zev has dispatched one of his own opponents, and John and Langley have dropped theirs. Down to just two and I have a feeling we don't want to get involved in those fights.

Elias gets the upper hand on his werewolf, grabbing its head in his powerful front paws and twisting. He drops the beast and staggers slightly. Not far from him, Zev has the other's throat in his jaws as he shakes it like a cat might shake a mouse. The werewolf is trying in vain to push Zev away with her claws or twist out of his grip. With one last, bone jarring shake, her neck snaps.

Zev drops her and immediately releases an adrenaline-fueled howl. Eli's voice raises in answer just before he collapses. Kalia and I rush for him, but John and Langley stop us.

"Don't go near him, he's not himself right now," Langley warns.

"Let me go," I answer through gritted teeth, wriggling free of his grip. I'm away again before he can grab me a second time.

I drop to my knees beside Elias to find him bleeding from several wounds. But the one that's caused him to fall is the one in his side, deep enough to see his ribs. "No, no, no, no, no. Shit!" I drop my pack and pull out a shirt, pressing it firmly against the wound in an attempt to stop the blood flow.

"Help me!" I order Langley.

He glances at Zev before meeting my gaze and shakes his head. Hot tears prick my eyes as helplessness floods through me. I follow Langley's look to Zev and find him staring at me, head cocked to one side and eyes glowing bright red. I realize then that Langley's actually afraid of him at this moment and I probably should be too. He's unlocked something inside himself that's more beast than man. I don't have the time to fear him right now, however. My best friend is dying and I'm not letting that happen without at least trying to save him.

I choke back a sob. "Dammit, Langley!" My voice breaks over rage filled tears. "At least throw me Zev's pack." He has the first aid kit, at the very least.

Something in my voice must alert Zev because he drops to all fours and pads silently towards me. John raises his gun and Zev ignores it. Gently, he bumps his head into me and nudges me aside. He sniffs Eli's wound and releases a low growl, turning a snarl at John and Langley.

John almost pulls the trigger, but Langley stays his hand. Seconds later, Zev is human again, though still snarling at the two men. "He needs stitches, now!" He growls at Langley.

Langley jumps into action as fast as if someone jabbed him in the ass with a hot fire poker. "Keep him steady." He tells Zev and me as he prepares needle and thread. We each take an arm and hold him down.

I can't stop the tears from falling now. Everything's slowed within him. His breathing's shallow and his heart beats are much too far apart. Worst of all, he's human again. That's never a good sign with injured werewolves.

I look at his closed eyes and place my forehead against his. "Don't leave me," I whisper to him. "I don't know how to do this without you." By 'this' I mean live. There isn't a time in my life I can remember where he wasn't just a call or text away. More often than not, he wasn't even that far. Zev's hand closes over mine, offering what comfort he can.

"I've done what I can," Langley tells us, rocking back on his haunches. "It's up to him now."

I sit back and dry my face with my hand. "You hear that, Elias Thorn? It's up to you. If you choose to die and leave me here alone, I promise when we meet again, I'm going to kick your ass." Maybe it's selfish of me to demand he stay, but I don't care. I still need him.

Langley moves off to tend to Sierra while Zev locates some clothes for himself and Eli and the others set about clearing away the bodies and digging out rations. Kalia comes to sit by me and loops her arm through mine, resting her head on my shoulder. "He'll stay," She says confidently.

"You think so?"

"I know so. He'd be an idiot to leave behind such a loyal friend, no matter who's waiting on the other side."

I chuckle a little. "If he stays, it'll be because he found out the sun walks on two legs and calls herself Kalia."

She giggles. "Or maybe he'll stay just to spite Zev."

We both laugh at that. "That sounds like him," I agree.

We sit together for a long time just watching him sleep. His breathing is deeper now, and his heartbeat is stronger. Maybe he'll stay after all.

John comes to make sure we eat and tells us to get some sleep.

132

Kalia stretches out beside Eli, placing her head near his heart. I give her some space, deciding to check on Sierra before going to sleep.

"How are you feeling?" I ask her.

"Terrified," she answers honestly. "All my life I've hated werewolves, and now I'm going to become one. How is that fair?"

I offer a smile. "It's not so bad. At least you've got Zev and Elias to show you the ropes."

She snorts. "Yeah, right. Zev would probably just watch and laugh as I meet my demise." She's probably right. I wouldn't blame him either. "This is your fault, by the way," she says.

"What did I do?"

"You told me you hoped I choked on my own poison."

I can't suppress my smile. "Oh yeah, I did do that." I know there's an evil glint in my eyes by the way Tony shifts uncomfortably and clears his throat.

"There's an antidote," he assures Sierra. "Don't worry, you just need to take it before the next full moon."

"It doesn't matter!" Zev snarls suddenly. He and Langley have been speaking in lowered voices to each other a little way from the group. Now, Zev's stalking into the woods.

"Zev, wait," Langley calls after him with no answer. He shakes his head and meets my gaze. I get the impression that I did something wrong, but I can't imagine what it was. He joins us at the fire.

"Is he alright?" I ask.

Langley looks into the fire with a sigh. "He's become an alpha and with that comes heightened emotions. Unfortunately, Zev is not good at handling emotions in any capacity. He just needs time to clear his head."

"Is it safe for him to be out there alone?"

He meets my eye with a pained look. "I don't know, Amane, is it?"

I search my instincts and shrug. "I don't sense anything threatening."

He turns back to the fire, the tension draining out of his shoulders. "Then we'll assume he's fine." The rest of us turn in to get some sleep while Langley keeps watch.

CHAPTER 18

When I wake next, the world is pitch dark beyond our fire. Zev and Langley are murmuring in low voices nearby.

"Have either of you slept yet?" I ask, drawing their attention.

"No," Zev answers simply, pointedly looking away from me. Seriously, what did I do?

"You should," I tell them. "You're still healing. I can take the watch."

"She's right," Langley agrees. "The day's not far off now."

Zev grunts his answer, sprawls on his back right where he is and closes his eyes. Langley smiles and shakes his head before finding a more comfortable location. I take his spot near the fire and open myself to my sixth sense.

"Langley said you could feel where Elias and I were in the village," Zev says quietly without opening his eyes.

"Yeah," I answer.

"How?"

I shrug. "I told you, you're important to me." He rolls onto his side, so his back is facing the fire and doesn't say another word. I don't have any other answer for him.

Elias is awake at dawn. He meets my eyes and smiles weakly but doesn't move for fear of waking Kalia. I move to sit beside him. "Hey, you made it back to us," I whisper.

"Where else would I go?" He asks.

"How do you feel?" I deflect the question.

"Sore, but alive. Was anyone else injured?"

Sierra was bitten. Everyone else just got some scratches."

He looks at where Zev's laying. "He's an alpha now." It's not a question.

"Apparently. I don't understand how that happened."

"Pure strength of will. He's immensely strong, Amane. I think even more so than Mingan. He's a true alpha, something Mingan never accomplished."

"Who's he the alpha of?"

"Us. His pack." He thinks about that for a minute and a sly smile quirks the corner of his mouth. "Maybe not *you*."

I frown. "What's that supposed to mean?" He shakes his head in answer.

Kalia stirs and opens her eyes. When she sees Eli's eyes open, she gasps and hugs him fiercely. "I knew you'd stay!"

He hugs her back and then winces. "Sorry," she says, quickly scrambling back.

"It's fine," he answers, reaching for her hand. "I'm going to get more sleep. Wake me when it's time to go."

"I don't think we're going far today," I tell him. He shrugs and settles back to sleep. I move back to the fire, leaving Kalia to watch over him.

"He lives?" Zev asks without moving.

"Yeah."

"Good." He sits, stretches, and then rises to disappear into the trees. Seems like the same old guarded Zev to me.

John and Langley decide to fashion a makeshift carrier for Eli, so we can keep moving. They're anxious to be out of the mountains now, and for good reason. Langley says the females that attacked last night were using some form of drug to increase their strength and stamina, which is why I couldn't seem to kill my opponent after putting way too many bullets in her. Langley seems to believe there may be other users in the area and wants to be well away before they realize we're here.

The men mostly alternate carrying the stretcher, though Kalia and I take a shift ourselves at one point. Eli seems to struggle to hold his tongue when Zev takes a shift with John. "Faster peons, you're king grows weary with this travel," he tells them cheerfully. Zev growls his response.

Eli looks up into his brother's face and a wicked smile quirks the corner of his mouth. I know what's coming, but can't shush him in time. "Sorry, ol' boy. Let me rephrase in a way you will understand. Mush!"

Zev stops in his tracks and the look he gives Eli is murderous. How much can he hurt his little brother without killing him? "Time to shut up," I tell Eli. "If he drops you, it will be your own fault."

Eli's eyes are locked on Zev as he nods. "Good call, Minny. My apologies, brother. I'm just going to sleep for a bit. Please, take your time." Zev scowls and starts moving again.

The remainder of our descent is uneventful. We locate the rest of our packs and weapons the following day. Elias refuses to be carried further, but Langley won't let him carry anything. We're about a day's travel from the van when Langley decides to ask what our plans are once this is over.

"We were kind of hoping we could stick around" Eli answers. "Become hunters ourselves."

"Really?" Langley asks, looking at me. "You want to be a hunter?"

I shrug. "I guess, or something in the business."

Sierra cackles evilly. "She wants to be a paper pusher."

I cringe at the idea. "Isn't there something in between the two. A position that allows you outside, but doesn't require so much killing?"

Kalia nods her agreement. "If there is, I want that too."

Langley chuckles. "I'm sure we can find a position for you."

"What about your homes and friends?" Kalia asks. "Won't you miss them?"

Elias shakes his head. "It was home because our family was there, and we never branched out much in the friend department. Our family is here now, so there's really nothing to go back to."

Zev stands abruptly and stalks away into the woods. Conversation pauses at this strange response, but Langley continues as though nothing has happened. "I'm sure there's some legalities to settle first. I will help with anything you need me to."

Eli and I smile at him gratefully. "Thanks!" We say in unison.

It's well past dark and the majority of our group is asleep, save John who's on duty, when Zev returns. I wake up to see him slipping soundlessly into camp. He quietly makes his way to my side and for a second, I think he's found something else to show me. Instead, he lays down beside me, settles on his side, and falls still. His back is to me, but he's so close I can feel the warmth of him. Strange for him to lay so close to anyone.

Because it's a cold night and he didn't take the time to unroll his own bedroll, I unzip mine and shift around until I manage to get it out from under me. Then I spread it out, so it covers both of us and back up, so our backs are pressed together. Otherwise, the full width of the sleeping bag still falls short by an inch or so.

I feel his muscles relax against me, so I guess he's ok with this invasion of his personal space. I know I certainly wouldn't be complaining about it on a night like this. Even so, I wish there was something between us and the ground.

I have the final watch before dawn and I use that time to flip through what's left of my parents' journals, looking for any part of them that isn't destroyed. It's a fruitless endeavor, more wishful thinking than anything. I'm halfway through the second one when Zev takes a seat beside me.

"Good morning, sunshine. I hope you slept well." I say. He simply grunts, so I return to flipping through pages.

I turn the last page and close the book before he finally speaks. "Do you love him?"

"Huh? Who?" I ask, completely lost.

"Elias."

"Oh, sure. Of course, I do. He's family."

"No, I mean... You once wanted something different from him. Do you still want that?"

I have no idea how Zev knows that. That is not a conversation I ever had, nor ever wanted to have with him. But now his question makes me stop and think. The truth is, at some point I'd stopped seeing Elias in any sort of romantic light. I couldn't say exactly when or why that changed, it just did.

"No, I don't. I am more than happy to call him brother."

"But you could track him to the village. That is a trait found mostly between a werewolf and his mate."

"Yeah, and I could track you also. Last I checked, we weren't mates either."

He pauses momentarily. It's the first time I've told anyone I could track Zev too. "I am his brother," he says thoughtfully. "We share blood, so maybe that's what you sensed. Just more of your mate's bloodline."

I let out a growl of frustration at his determination to spin Eli and me as a couple. Taking his chin in my hand, I turn his head, so he sees where Eli and Kalia are snuggled up together. "He is not my mate. If anything, he is Kalia's, and I know that's just as obvious to you as the rest of the world. You may be half blind, but you're not stupid."

I release him. "I don't know why you keep insisting that he and I are a couple, or why it matters to you enough to keep bringing it back up."

I watch as he begins several replies, only to discard them and start again. Finally, he stands, growling out, "Never mind," before stalking away. I watch him go, feeling completely confused. When I look away, I find Langley watching us, looking thoroughly amused. My answering look is one of bewilderment.

Langley joins me by the fire. "I don't understand what his problem is." I tell Langley. "Did I do something wrong? Is he just concerned I'm not good enough for his brother?"

Langley chuckles. "No, not at all. He's concerned that he isn't good enough for what *he* wants, actually. So, in typical Zev fashion, he has put up walls and made excuses as to why it's beyond his reach."

"Why would Elias being my mate keep them from a solid relationship?"

He gives me a long, measuring look. "You and Zev both seem to think the world is overlooking you on its way to more interesting things. It's almost aggravating.

"Listen, you're probably aware of this, but when a werewolf chooses a mate, it's for life. Elias and Kalia, that's written in the stars now. Zev has neither his brother's confidence, nor his ability with words. He has this almost debilitating belief that he will never measure up. In his mind, he will never be good enough for the one his heart has already claimed as his mate. So, he pushes when he should hold on and he's silent when he should speak, and he storms off when he gets too close to the truth."

There's an understanding poking at the back of my mind, but I'm afraid to acknowledge it. "Ok, I'm not sure I follow."

Langley smiles. "I'm sure you do, you're just not sure you want to. Amane, by the time Zev gets up the nerve to say what he's really feeling we may all be old and dead. Now, I don't know what you may feel towards him, but I suggest you tell him what it is before he stops talking altogether."

I nod and he leaves me to mull over his words. Zev chose me? When? Why? Why not another werewolf? How does Langley know this when the better part of mine and Zev's interactions have been cordial at best? And why does this knowledge make my heart hammer against my ribs and my stomach swim with butterflies?

The more I think about it, the more obvious the answers become. Certain looks and conversations take on new meaning in my awareness. Feelings I've suppressed because I couldn't handle new feelings along with all the emotions I've been experiencing.

I become steadily more jittery until I can't sit still any longer. I shove the journals back into Zev's bag and head off into the woods. I don't know what I'm going to say to him. I can't really think straight at the moment beyond finding him.

He's not far, sitting by a stream and looking totally lost in thought. I take a seat next to him and he doesn't even acknowledge me. Maybe Langley's wrong and I'm about to make an idiot of myself.

I'm not really sure how to begin. "It's a little early for such deep thoughts, Mr. Atlas."

"I think it's a little early for a lot of things," he answers without looking at me. Such an answer could be interpreted in so many ways.

I hug my knees to my chest and look towards the rising sun. "Perhaps you're right."

For a long time, we just sit and listen to the burbling water and the song of Spring birds. It's going to be another beautiful day. Part of me is sad we'll be going back underground tonight, closed away from nature once more.

"I'm sorry." Zev breaks the silence. "It wasn't fair of me to make those assumptions about you and Elias."

I shrug it off. "You're not the first. You should know, however, that Elias has always found the idea to be gross."

"Elias is an idiot," he says, still not looking at me.

"We all have our tendencies." I give a half-assed attempt at defending Eli. Zev grunts.

I sigh and place my chin on my knees. Now what? I've never done this before. Do I just blurt out my feelings and hope for the best? I don't have all day. Any minute now, he's going to decide we should head back, and my chance will be lost.

"I hate to interrupt, but we're ready to go." Eli's voice breaks in. And there goes my chance.

Zev doesn't hesitate to get away from me. I'm pretty certain Langley's wrong about his reasons behind asking about Eli and me. He brushes past Eli without a second look. "Did I interrupt something?" Eli asks, confused.

I shake my head. "I honestly don't know. It's been an odd morning."

Spirits are high again today, with the end of our trip in sight. I think we're all looking forward to good food and real beds. Kalia drops back to hook arms with me and we skip a little, giggling when we trip over roots. Sierra joins on Kalia's other side and we all try to walk in step like a bunch of tween girls.

Elias and Tony eventually drop back to retrieve their ladies, which somehow turns into the four of them racing around the woods with the girls shrieking. At least we won't be disturbed by any wildlife today.

The van comes into view just right around dusk. Sierra and Kalia skip ahead enthusiastically, the rest of us following a bit slower. All of us, except Zev, who has come to halt in the trees. I turn to make sure he's ok and find him just staring at the van for some reason.

"Zev, are you coming?" I ask. He looks at me and then off into the woods with a shrug. Ahead, Eli stops to investigate, but Langley urges him onward.

I walk back to stand before Zev. "Are you ok?"

"Yeah," he answers, looking me in the eyes for the first time since that morning. The look makes my stomach wiggle, but I can't read what's behind it.

"Just decided you prefer sleeping on the ground instead of a nice bed?" I ask with a teasing smile.

Another shrug. "I prefer the company I've shared while sleeping on the ground."

I wrinkle my nose. "If you enjoyed it that much, I'm sure we can get Sierra to sleep in your general vicinity once in a while."

He almost smiles, but he's giving me a really intense look. "You're really looking forward to being underground again?"

My own smile fades and I glance at my feet. "I guess it depends on who will be there. Like, I don't know, I suppose..." I draw a breath, preparing myself for what I'm about to say and the rejection I'm certain will follow. "I think it will really suck if you're not there."

He gives me a long, searching look. My stomach clenches in a knot, certain I just made an ass of myself. "I think the woods might really suck if you're not here."

I can't hide my smile. Does this mean... "So, can we at least go to headquarters tonight? I will willingly wander the woods with you any day, but I am in desperate need of a shower, and I want a warm bed."

He smiles back at me, bright and beautiful. He holds out a hand for me to shake. "Deal." He does like me!

I accept, binding him to the agreement. There's still uncertainty in my thoughts. Could Langley really be right about how werewolves pick mates? We haven't known each other very long at all. He's barely opened up at all to me. How can that be good for a sustainable relationship?

"Just, please don't shut me out anymore, ok?" I ask in a quiet voice. It feels as though I'm asking the world of him after what happened in the village.

He's quiet, for a long time. Maybe he's thinking better of this whole thing. Better to be alone and unbothered, most likely. He surprises me by reaching his hand out once more, resting it on my cheek this time, and drawing me into him. My mind blanks, closing in on just this moment here and now as our lips meet in a physical display of a promise not yet spoken. "I will do my best not to," he answers quietly, our faces still so close I can count his lashes. I smile at him, knowing this is the best he can offer, and relieved he's willing to make such an offer at all.

At the van, we're met by an exasperated Sierra. "It's about time," she says from the back seat. "I thought I was going to grow old waiting for you two to get down here."

"Sorry," I tell her. "Zev was worried he might miss you once we get back." I notice Eli's gaze take in Zev and me before he catches my eye. A small smile lights his face and he winks. A blush creeps over my face as I climb into my seat.

Sierra is making a face somewhere between disgust and embarrassment at my comment. "Don't worry. I set him straight," I tell her as Zev settles in beside Eli.

CHAPTER 19

Over the next week, Langley makes it his business to help us settle our affairs back home. The police have been looking for us to make a report, a memorial needs to be set up for our parents and Eli's house needs to be emptied and evaluated. According to Dorris's will, the house and most everything in it is now Eli's. I'm surprised to find she left me her weapons and some odds and ends. I figured it would all go to Eli.

There's nothing left of my house. It burned long and hot that night. I stand in the driveway for a long time just taking in the blackened area, Zev and Eli flanking me like silent sentinels.

After days of sorting through the charred remains, the crews did manage to uncover three incredibly valuable, yet priceless items. My father's swords. When the authorities place them into my hands, I weep tears of joy. Here is a connection not just to my parents, but to all my ancestors who came before. I hadn't wanted to admit that mere objects held so much meaning, or that the loss of them had felt like losing a connection I could not bear to lose.

There's a larger turnout for the memorial than I anticipated. A lot of our parent's old friends come to ground thanks to Langley getting the word out. There are a lot of tears shed, especially from Elias and Langley. Kalia came with us from headquarters, so she is here to hold Eli while Zev lends what comfort he can to Langley.

I remain mysteriously dry-eyed, making me wonder at my own numbness. It's hard for me to wrap my head around the fact that we're here in town and our parents are not, and never will be again. Almost like their entire existence was a dream, or the series of events that followed their deaths was a dream. But Zev and Langley and Kalia are here, telling me the trip was real, and the emptiness that seems to cover the world tells me my parents were also real.

We hold a reception at Eli's house after and I accept condolences without feeling. I simply go through the motions of thanking people for coming. I don't miss the puzzled looks my lack of expression draws from our guests.

After a while, I retreat to Eli's room. Downstairs, there are too many emotions, and none of them are mine. I'm like an empty shell where others' emotions have decided to coalesce.

Eventually, Eli appears beside me as I stare blankly across a yard we spent years playing in. "How are you holding up?" He asks.

"Do you think I'm broken?" I answer with my own question.

"No, why would you think you're broken?"

"I'm just... Numb inside. Shouldn't I feel something? Anything?"

He wraps an arm around my shoulders and pulls me against his side. "I think your mistake is believing there's any type of shoulds or should nots in this situation. Everyone grieves differently and in their own time. You're not broken, Minny."

"I hope you're right."

A knock on the door pulls us around to find Kalia and Zev in the doorway. "Sorry," Kalia says. "We just wanted to let you know that guests are beginning to leave."

"Shall we say our farewells?" Eli asks me.

"You go ahead. I'll be right down." I tell him. He gives me another squeeze and then leaves, hand in hand with Kalia. I turn back to the window to finish gathering myself before facing people again. Zev joins me, hands in his pockets as he takes in the view. He's still awkward about touching me sometimes, not quite believing that I want it as much as he does.

"I used to hide up here when we were little if we argued about something. It's his room, but I would commandeer it. From up here, I could watch him rage around the yard until he was ready to apologize." I smile at the memory. "He would always apologize, even when it was my fault, just so I'd talk to him again."

Zev doesn't answer, but gently brushes my hair behind my ear, his hand lingering near my neck. For a second, he just studies me, and then leans forward to kiss my temple. These quiet gestures of understanding are just one of the reasons he's captured my heart so completely. He knows without any explanation that I'm reminiscing about more than childish arguments.

After everyone's left and the sun has set, when it's just our core group once more, we light a fire in the yard. I bring out the journals and pass one to Elias. As one we add them to the fire, our final farewell to the people who loved us like no one ever will again.

As I watch the covers curl, and the pages disintegrate, the dam inside me finally breaks. Weeks of suppressing my emotions are undone in seconds. They pour out in ugly, wrenching sobs as I finally face the reality that my parents are gone, and they are never coming back. Zev holds me tight, and I relax into him. He doesn't try to ease my pain with words. He just stands there and lets me lean on him.

There's too much swirling around my head later that night for sleep to be an option. I creep out of bed, careful not to wake Kalia. We have been sharing Dorris's bed while we are here. Stepping out onto the porch, I'm not surprised to find Elias already sitting on the steps. I take a seat beside him and look up at the stars. The moon has begun waxing once more. In the woods behind the house the peepers are chirping noisily and an owl hoots in the distance.

"Trouble sleeping?" Eli asks.

"Yeah, just… Busy thoughts."

He's quiet for a moment, and then, "Do you think they'd be disappointed in our choices?"

I think about it before answering. "No, I think they'd be really proud of us. I think we've done a lot of growing in a very short time and I think they'd see that."

"I hope so." Another pause. "Do you think Mom would have liked Kalia?"

"Are you kidding me? How could anyone *not* like her? She's polite, cheerful and incredibly sweet all the time. Your mom would have loved her, hands down."

He smiles. "I think you're right."

"I know I am." I frown then. "Dad would have hated Zev, though."

He considers this. "Maybe, at first. But then he'd see how he weirdly makes you happy, and how he'd willingly give his life for you, and then he wouldn't care anymore. He never objected too much as long as you were safe and happy."

He's right. Dad could be a total pushover if it meant I would smile. Mom wouldn't have needed convincing. She always loved everyone unless given a reason not to.

Elias stands and stretches. "I should get to bed. I'm exhausted. Don't stay up too late, Minny. We have another long day tomorrow."

"I won't," I answer. "Have a good night."

"Yeah, you too." He pauses in the doorway. "Oh, and Minny?" I turn to see him smiling like he's got a secret. "I love you too."

End

Printed in the United States
by Baker & Taylor Publisher Services